The Flirty Felon

 ROMANCING A THORNE

RIA ZEN

Cover Photo: Volodymyr Bahrii
Book Editing: Lisa Lee Proofreading and Editing

First Edition
Paperback ISBN 978-1-990588-03-7
eBook ISBN 978-1-7770780-8-9

Chapter 1

Jaxson froze in place when he spotted her. He could have from miles away. How could he forget her dark braids, punk clothes, or the way she leaned on her right foot when she was daydreaming? How tempting it would be to sneak up behind her, poke her in the ribs, and pull her into an embrace.

Genesis was his first love. One look at her and he could remember the taste of her lips and the decadent thoughts her chocolate gaze gave him. But she was with another man, and that man had to be in one of the adjacent aisles in the hardware store. So Jaxson stood there in the gardening section, clutching the spade, refraining from spouting out a 'hoe' joke, when those dangerous eyes turned to him.

Their relationship had ended nearly a year ago, yet before it had, he had mistakenly made the decision in his heart to marry her.

"Jax?" Genesis peeked around then skipped towards him. As she stepped closer, he stepped back. "How are you?"

He lifted the metal spade with a rubber gripped handle which he planned to charge to his employer, Mr. and Mrs. Walters, and avoided more eye-contact than he had already given. They needed this space, more for him than her. She seemed perfectly fine to move on to the next pretty face.

"Are we good or not?"

Jaxson rubbed his lips together.

"I'm really happy for you. It would have been difficult to find a job when you're—I'm proud of you. Starting over. Cleaning up. It can't be easy."

"It isn't," he mumbled, eyeing the garden tools again. He was giving every effort to not call her that particular one with the long handle and a metal blade at the end. He would not tear her apart the way she had him, leaving him to cry every night alone in his jail cell. With a heavy exhale, he finally dared to face her, knowing he could not move on if he was unable to look her in the eye. "But it builds character."

"I never pictured you to be a gardener." She smiled, easing the tension with a subtle twitch in her cheek. "I would fail miserably."

"That's why they hired me and not you," he said far too naturally, mirroring her grin.

"Genesis?" her boyfriend, Ezekiel, called out.

"I should go." She slipped out her phone. "Do you have a new number? I forgot to ask at Zeke's staff party last week. Even though we… if you ever want to talk, we can still be friends."

Friends. The word sucker punched him in the gut.

"No phone." Jaxson stepped around her, carrying the spade to the cash register, bumping her gently in the process. It was instinct and he immediately regretted it.

The cashier stared at him like there was more than the one item. It was a look he got often.

Jaxson eyed the lighters, something he'd often slip into his pocket when his buddies would ask for smokes, but the past was behind him—just like Genesis.

"Actually," he walked over to the seed packets, "never mind." July was too late in the season to plant new flowers and the blossoms he stared at brought back too many painful memories. He paid cash, then tucked the receipt into his cargo shorts, leaving the store abruptly.

When he returned to the Walters' estate, their youngest daughter, Brooklyn, waved at him through the window. Minutes later, as he was hunched over a weed-infested flower bed along the edge of his employer's acreage, she appeared.

"Need anything?" he asked politely, mustering up whatever willpower he had left to keep his bitter words to himself. Brooklyn had never worked a day of physical labor in her life.

"I wanted to help." She picked up the trowel, and meticulously flicked the dirt off the edge with her floral gloved fingers. "Like my outfit? I'm dressed for the job, so it's okay if I get a little dirty." She winked.

He shivered.

Still she proceeded to squat to his level in a loose tank top and powder pink shorts. "The hat is new too, you like it?"

"I don't need your help." Jaxson sighed. "This is my job. Please go back and do whatever you were doing before."

Brooklyn groaned, "But I like spending time with you."

"You shouldn't. You should pretend I don't exist and let me do my job."

"Well aren't you in a sour mood. It's summer and I'm your boss, and I think you've done enough today. It's so hot out. Have a break."

"I just returned."

She pouted her lips, then walked away. Jaxson sighed with relief, until a shock of ice cold water shot him in the back. His tank top clung to his skin. He wanted to throw it off, but that is exactly what Brooklyn expected him to do, so he held his ground.

"Much better."

Jaxson clenched his fists, seething as he turned on his heel.

She sprayed him again. This time in the face, cackling. "What? It's just a little innocent fun." But it wasn't. She watered the flowerbed he was weeding. The soil thickened like mud, when it was like sand moments ago, easy to shake out unwanted plants.

"How many times do I have to tell you? No!" he growled, "Your sister is marrying my brother."

"Yeah, but we're not related."

"But we will be," Jaxson griped. Not once in the months he had been caring for the estate had he shown any remote interest in his future sister-in-law. Unlike every other guy on the planet, he saw her more as an annoying girl than the datable diva. Her blonde hair and blue eyes didn't fool him. "And you're not my boss, your parents are. They gave me this job—not you, which I am forever grateful for." Once he was in her proximity, he reached for the garden hose, and rewrapped it against its stand. "I need this job. I don't have any other options, so stop making this miserable for me. Even if Jesse never dated Collette, you need to understand, I am not looking for love."

Brooklyn stepped towards him, and he stepped backwards, until they were at the edge of their outdoor pool. Her eyebrow twitched with a glint of mischief, and she pushed him in.

Jaxson's back slammed into the water surface, like breaking through a thin sheet of ice on this blistering hot day. He paddled to the surface, coughing out the drops of water that he accidentally inhaled on his fall.

"All I wanted was some fun."

"No. You wanted to play with me like I'm your toy, and I'm not." He paddled to the edge and climbed out. "Girls are all the same, doesn't matter how pretty they are, the bane of their existence is to torture me." He tugged up his shorts, and flicked the excess water trickling down his sun-kissed skin. "I am not here to flirt, I am here to work, something you have never done a day in your spoiled life."

Her mouth gaped. "I am not... I can't help that my parents are successful and yours weren't."

"Never," Jaxson growled, his voice was extra coarse from the choking fit, "never talk smack about people you've never met." He wanted to cuss her out, but he held great restraint. If he was going to fit into everyday society, he had to show restraint. He whistled out a tightened breath, realizing his anger crossed the line. "This isn't about the money. I'm falling behind on my tasks because I am constantly interrupted by an annoying girl who shouldn't be flirting with me. So let me say this clearly. Hands to yourself, don't talk to me, and stop trying. It is never going to happen. Get a job, get a hobby, I don't care—just leave me alone."

"But I'm bored."

"Then do something that isn't boring. Go hang out with a friend or something. I don't care as long as you go away."

"But…"

"Stop. Before you say there's a push and pull, hot and cold thing going on, there isn't. Stop before I truly say harsh words."

"Another late night?" Melanie asked her brother, as he plopped a Styrofoam takeout container on her lap. He dug through the paper bag, and tossed the wooden chopsticks at her. "Hey! Aim!"

She missed the catch, so she had to fish for them around the cushions.

Bryson sat in the recliner next to her and kicked up his legs, "Yeah. I was going to pull a late night at the firm, but I didn't want to leave my sister to fend for herself with her first day of work tomorrow."

"I'm touched." She split the chopsticks apart and rubbed them between her palms and popped open the number six special from the Chinese restaurant a block away. "Thanks for cooking." She pinched a mouthful and slurped the chow mien noodles whimsically. "Maybe one of these days you'll actually use your kitchen."

"Can't. It's too dusty. I thought having you as a roommate meant I would have someone to use it for me, maybe help around the place and take care of me."

"That would be a wife."

Bryson laughed, then pointed his chopsticks at her when she realized how awful her innocent joke turned out.

"I didn't mean it like that."

"Oh, and what did you mean?" Bryson snickered, shoving his gob with noodles.

"I was implying you subconsciously take on the traditional roles of man versus woman. Man works hard in the office, and the women you tend to be attracted to just happen to be quite domestic, something which I am not. Hospitable sure, but you cook bacon better than I ever will. Women can be just as established if not more established than you, Bryson. Some of us actually want to work."

"What are you watching?" Obviously her brother didn't want to dive into the subject of women. He had struggled in the area of relationships, but hey, at least he tried.

"Just channel surfing." She shrugged, unsure of the emotions swirling inside her. She should have been stirring with excitement, but something seemed off. "Can't decide on anything."

"Do you feel ready?" Bryson wasn't in his usual suit and tie, but a navy polo shirt and khaki pants, meaning he had most likely spent all day in the office. They shared a lot of features. Both were slim body types, had dark narrow eyes, and naturally straight hair. His was jet-black like their father's and trimmed short. He never allowed himself to grow a beard, not that it would fill out much if he tried, and it seemed he had doubled his hours at the gym since the last time she was in this town. Unlike her, he was blessed with height.

At least she was taller than her mom.

Moving in to his apartment seemed like the right choice. She was excited to catch up with him this summer without the pressure of nursing school or a returning flight. Melanie and Bryson had always had a close relationship, so it felt like they'd been apart for too long, with him settling his roots into this law firm, and her off at university. They hadn't had lazy moments like this in a long time.

"As ready as I'll ever be. They already gave me the tour. I aced the interview, and they sound excited to have me. I kind of wish I was working in a different section of the building, but maybe after a couple years of this, I could bump up to the main wing. The staff seems cool, but working in the ER is going to be stressful." She glanced down at the savory dish, stabbing into a piece of extra chewy, extra sweet ginger beef. "Do you feel ready for court?"

"Always." He chomped onto his spring roll, burning his mouth, then gasped. Reaching into the bag he cracked open an ice cold green tea, then grinned proudly at her. "I'm glad you chose to live here."

"I would choose living with you over Mom or Dad any day." She decided to cut off her comment there, and not mention he may have needed her too. She knew something was off when he skipped Christmas, to find out his longtime girlfriend moved on. She didn't know the details of what happened, which seemed strange to her. Usually he opened up to her about nearly everything, so she figured something was up. This breakup hit him hard. It was a shock to her too. Collette Walters didn't seem like a heartbreaker. There was something about this, he was refusing to tell her, but Melanie figured if she waited patiently, he would open up to her eventually. It was part of the reason she moved to this town. It wasn't like it was her only option. Nurses were needed all around the country.

Their dad paid for her schooling and the post graduation trip afterwards. She had no intention of flying overseas to live in a densely overpopulated country like Hong Kong. Closer to him or not, he still wouldn't give her or any of them the time of day. His love came in the form of a trust fund.

If their mom didn't want to emigrate why would she? Then again their mother was on the other side of the country, also in a metropolitan city and Melanie was never a fan of the elite social circles her lifestyle had either.

The simplicity of town life attracted her as it did Bryson. There she could be whomever she wanted and view the world like her classmates. It was important she could prove to her family and herself, that she didn't need her parent's money. It meant more than anything, that she had the freedom to make her own choices and friends.

"Maybe you could visit the office sometime." Bryson finished his spring roll. "You will like my coworker, Rhett. He's smart and talented—not as much as me of course, but he's pretty darn close. Second best lawyer in the office." He chuckled. "He always has the best jokes. I'd tell you the one he shared today, but I would give it no justice. You'll have to hear it from him. I really think you'd like him. We're about the same in age and—"

"Unbelievable!" Melanie stood, taking her container with her to her room. She slammed the door and locked it. "I don't want to date any of your lawyer friends." She looked to the ceiling, and slowly slid to the ground. In a softer voice she added, "I don't want the doctors or city real estate agents either." She thought about all the 'eligible bachelors' their mom tried to set her up with when she returned home for the holidays. "I want to live life and not have to worry about the prestige."

In her heart she felt the pressure to outperform her peers. As a child it was all about her grades and what classes she took. Now as an adult, it was what man she was seen with, and she'd had enough. What was the point of living if it was dictated for her? She had already completed her bachelor's in nursing a year early thanks to an accelerated program. What would satisfy them? Nothing would make them stop, but Bryson?

They were supposed to be on the same team. Brother and sister looking out for each other. The last thing Melanie wanted was for Bryson to act just like their parents. This was supposed to be her escape.

Yes their parents had sacrificed everything when they immigrated to the country, starting from the ground up, like eons ago, but when would it ever be enough? They went from zero to millions, but her path didn't revolve around numbers. She didn't need people looking out for her anymore. It was her turn to take a hold of her life.

"Mel," Bryson called out. He pounded on the door. "You haven't met him, please. I promised him already."

"You what?" she roared, "I promised nothing. Why don't you date him, if you like him so much?"

"Melanie! You owe me this."

"I owe you nothing. You invited me to stay here and I accepted. Gifts aren't debts."

"I just want my baby sister to be happy."

"Do you want me to be happy, or do you want a distraction from the fact you're not happy? You have to move on. When I'm ready to find happiness, I'll chase it. It's not up to you to worry about me, worry about yourself."

"I do worry about you."

"I'm not sick anymore," she said, reflecting on her childhood when she had missed a year of school due to illness. It was her experience that inspired her to become what she was today, a woman on the front lines, a nurse. "Bryson, maybe you fix up your own life before adding to mine."

She felt a thud on the other side of the door and her brother's heavy sigh, "It's too late for me. I threw away something great."

"Three years though, you may not have married her, but you'll have the friendship that remains."

"No," he sighed again, "Even if she didn't hate my guts, Jesse, her fiancé, does—and before you say it, I don't have any intention on befriending him either. And it was two and a half."

"Whoa, big difference." She rolled her eyes. "This is why you should move on. Once you are content, in love or not, you won't have jealousy preventing you from salvaging a worthwhile friendship."

"I sent his brother, Jaxson, to jail." The flooring beneath his feet creaked. "And I don't regret it."

"Oh." That would have to be a blow to his ego. While Melanie pushed herself to the place she was, Bryson pushed harder. Any setback he would curse himself for, aiming to double her successes shortly after. It must have worried him that his affluent ex-girlfriend would have a familial connection to the system. From what she remembered of her, Collette was a patient woman, but how far off did the apple fall from the tree? How different would her fiancé, Jesse, be from the criminal? To her understanding, most criminals had poor decision making skills, often taking domestic matters and turning them into more severe circumstances. Like two people who couldn't get along had the potential to escalate to homicide. Having someone dangerous like that near the woman he loved must have been awfully difficult on her brother's broken heart. It probably took a heavy toll on his conscience too.

"Collette's fiancé isn't any better. Those Thorne boys are trouble. Jaxson is a convicted criminal, and Jesse is… irritating." The change in his tone startled her. She should have never reopened the sore wound, if she was preaching, he needed to heal. "If I could send him back to jail, I would in a heartbeat, taking Jesse down too."

"What did he do?"

"What didn't he do?" he snapped back.

"If you don't answer me, I'm going to assume you hate him because you're acting childish and won't admit your feelings of jealousy are corrupting your views of innocent people."

"He called me out in front of her whole family. I've been the laughing stock, the butt end of the joke ever since." Bryson punched the wall, "And he messed with my car!"

Again Melanie rolled her eyes. "You still sound jealous." Maybe if he gave half the amount of care and attention he did to his ex like he had his car, they would've been married by now. "And who is this Jesse?"

"He's an immature mammoth with tattoos down both arms. The bloke looks like he belongs in a biker gang, but they work together at Price Event Rentals. He drives the delivery truck and when he is in the office, had nothing better to do than pester Collette. I could write a whole book on the awful pranks he pulled on her." As he spoke, she looked up his profile online.

Ah. So he had a low-end job and an appearance he didn't approve of. Yeah, she could see why her brother was irked. But hey, some girls were into the rough and tough lumberjack type. He was possibly the polar opposite to Bryson.

"And he won her over with a cat."

"That's adorable."

Bryson scowled. He was allergic to cats. His skin would turn red and his face would swell if he tried petting one.

"Hey, does Brooklyn still live in town?" she asked, changing the subject, since it was clearly a heated one. Brooklyn had texted her while Bryson had been rambling on, plus Melanie had been itching to reconnect with her. She never thought she would develop such a strong bond to Collette's younger sister. They had met a previous summer when Melanie was only visiting Bryson, which wasn't much of a visit considering Collette would also be there. Thus Melanie and Brooklyn became instant best friends or the closest thing if school and distance wasn't pulling them apart.

"Brooklyn?" his voice changed again, from anger to confusion. "Oh. I haven't thought about her. Yeah, she still lives with her parents, uptown, why?"

"She invited me over... to bird watch?" Melanie said puzzled by the text message. Was this the same Brooklyn she remembered? She was certain bird watching was at the bottom of the list of things her glam girl would ever show an interest for. Unless by 'birds' she meant boys, she must have had the wrong number.

Chapter 2

"Are we going to stare at your gardener all day?" Melanie asked, perched at the bay window next to her friend. The shirtless man had their back to them, giving them the perfect view of his tanned deltoids. There were a few scribbles of ink along them, but as long as he didn't turn his face around, she justified this as an objective observation.

"Yes." Brooklyn giggled. "Popcorn?"

"You're not serious are you?" His muscles flexed at each snip with the hedge trimmers. She thought herself as a modest woman, yet the only thing pure was the constant gusts of lust coursing through her veins. She resorted to a collapsible fan to steady her fever.

"Definitely."

"We'll get so fat." Ashamed, Melanie covered the blush in her cheeks with the turquoise fan, contrasting her dark eyes. The gardener had to be close to her age, which was a dangerous thought on its own.

Men were so far off her radar when it came to moving to town, but it was a hopeless cause for her to avert her gaze from this hard-working man, so much strength and energy bursting from each movement. He oozed power and fecundity—formidability. Thank goodness no one could read her mind.

"Impossible," Brooklyn said, scanning Melanie's petite figure, then her own womanly curves. Melanie dreamed for a body like her friend's, and could easily see why she was often hired by local businesses to assist in their social media campaigns. "Maybe I'll cut up some watermelon instead." She tapped her magenta lips, "When he walks over to the vegetable garden, I'll find some baskets so we can pick some fruit. Mom wants me to make jam with the plums."

"Do you even know how?"

"No," she cackled, "Collette does though."

Brooklyn excused herself to the kitchen, but Melanie remained perched at the bay window, secretly admiring the chestnut haired boy—no, he was most definitely a man, and she had to stop thinking like this, like she was no longer a little girl, but a woman who wanted a man. She exhaled, fanning faster.

The gardener picked up the water hose and sprayed the base of the hedges. When he was done, he spritzed water into the air, and combed his damp wavy hair back, and it molded to his scalp like his palm was full of hair gel.

Brooklyn returned with a tray of sliced fruits and napkins. She lowered the plate between them, deciding to sit cross-legged in front of her friend.

"What happened to the other guy?"

"Retired." Brooklyn sighed, admiring the replacement. "We've had him around since January. Everything outside is his responsibility, the yard, the garden, driveway, the pool, pathways—he's meticulous. Here I was excited Mom and Dad were hiring a bad boy, but he's been nothing but… but… perfect." She chomped into her watermelon slice.

Melanie held hers to her lips, watching him wind up the garden hose. With his worn out cap flipped backwards, and grass stained shorts, he did have a tough-guy look to him.

"He told me I couldn't watch him anymore. It doesn't mean you can't." She waggled her eyebrows, clearly up to no good. "He told me to hang out with a friend."

Melanie laughed. Of course Brooklyn tried to hit on him, and knowing her, she must have been awfully persistent.

"Friend meet Jaxson."

"Jaxson?" Melanie choked on her fruit. She quickly wiped away the juices. She preferred not knowing his name, the less connection the better, and in this case, way better. Surely Jaxson was a common name, it wasn't that Jaxson, the one fresh on her mind was it?

"Yes. Jaxson, as in Jesse's younger brother."

"Well no wonder he won't date you. Brooklyn, you can't date your future brother-in-law. That's just weird." And maybe it was better off this way, considering he was a convict!

"It's been done before."

Melanie fluttered her eyelashes in irritation. There was no use in reasoning with her friend. She remembered when Brooklyn sent her texts about Jesse around the time he was maybe-dating-maybe-just-crushing on her older sister, which only made the situation weirder. Yes, the Thorne boys were hot, Jaxson case and point, but it was wrong to hit on him. Melanie wasn't going to. He was checkout-his-Instagram-profile cute. He was not she-could-utter-a-coherent-sentence-around-him enchanting. She had been too focused on her studies and avoiding arranged marriages the last few years to remember how to flirt successfully. Remember how to stop the bleeding after a bullet wound or master chest compressions, sure. Talk to hot guys? System failure. Her heart nearly malfunctioned, when he turned around.

"Is he single?" *Please say no. Please make this a million times easier on me before I embarrass myself.*

Brooklyn nodded enthusiastically, "Just out of a bad breakup too. Look." She pointed at him at the moment he was walking towards them on a brick path. He had a wide jaw, and the makings of a young beard, though his sunglasses covered nearly half his face.

Spotting the two of them, his brows furrowed. He turned abruptly towards the fruit and vegetable garden.

"Hurry." Brooklyn shoved Melanie, "Hurry! It's the heat of the day. He's going to go home soon."

"Isn't he staying at that little house by the garage?" Melanie followed her to the patio, rushing to slip on their sandals.

"Yes, but Daddy said if I surprised him again, he wouldn't take me to Niagara Falls. It's already bad enough we're not going to Venice this year." She rolled her eyes. "Saving up for the wedding. Whatever. I won't get to see Fabio."

"Fabio as in the Italian Jaxson?"

Brooklyn giggled. "I missed you."

She squeezed her friend in a hug, mainly to slow her down. If this was the same Jaxson Bryson was talking about, he was indeed a dangerous guy. Her brother would never prosecute an innocent man. Her suspicions were confirmed when they reached him.

"We came to help pick strawberries." Brooklyn gleamed.

"They're not ripe enough," Jaxson said in a gravelly voice. "If you pick them too early, they'll stay sour. Give them another two days."

"Well then what can I do?"

"Hang out with your friend." He nodded once, acknowledging Melanie but it was guarded. Not a smirk, or offering his hand, he instead took a step back, distancing himself farther from her.

Melanie didn't need anyone to tell her, she knew when she wasn't welcome, so she too took a step back. She tried to read more into him, but the sun shone above his head, forcing her to look away.

"Bugs are getting—I'll head out." Melanie stuttered an excuse. She couldn't understand why her heart raced. How a subtle nod could cause her to feel like she was in a hostile situation. If only she could read his eyes, then she could truly evaluate if the man was as dangerous as she originally perceived, or if it was her brother's words clouding her judgment.

"Can't chat. Your parents decided to host an engagement party for Jesse and Collette tomorrow night," Jaxson said shortly after Brooklyn's friend walked away, not giving her another glance.

"That's sudden." Brooklyn gripped her arm bashfully. She too could sense the chill in the air from her parents' actions.

"Yeah, even your sister doesn't know what's happening." It was nowhere near enough time for Jesse to properly inform his friends, but that was probably the point. The Walters loved that their daughter was happy. They didn't however like why.

Jaxson would forever be grateful for Collette's kindness, and the bail money she used to pull him out of jail. She had begged her parents to help him find work; however, it didn't mean he or his brother were welcomed into the family with open arms.

The Thorne boys didn't fit into their perfect little box.

The Walters never struggled like them. They never had to worry about if they missed the school bus, they missed school, or if their mom could afford her medications, especially when she had to quit work, because her health made it impossible for her to continue. Even if she persisted, her body failed her. They never had to wonder if she could. Would she still be alive or would her cancer have progressed anyway?

No, the Walters saw the Thorne boys as two tall bouncers etched in tattoos and as societal failures. While at times they were gracious to him, there were times Jaxson would never fit in, neither would Jesse. They wouldn't lift their noses high to their peers, iron their shirts, or waste an afternoon golfing. In their eyes, Jesse was a poor boy, too pitiful to be understood—which couldn't be further from the truth.

"She will figure it out quick," he added. With Collette and Jesse working at Price Event Rentals, the Walters were bound to rent a few things. Jaxson hadn't seen the list, but the news alone had doubled his workload for the day.

"What suit are you wearing?"

"What suit?" Jaxson laughed, "It's summer. It's outside." It was at the Walters' main estate. Okay, yeah, he wouldn't have a choice. He was going to wear a suit.

"Knowing Mom, she will have photographers, so I'm going to call my hairdresser for the both of us, but you're also shaving."

Jaxson stroked his scruff.

"It looks better on Jesse than it does you. Hair wise, it will only be a trim. I like the long hair, but it needs expert attention."

"You're unbearable."

"You're welcome." She blew a kiss in his direction, but he dodged it, pivoting on his heel. Brooklyn immediately rushed inside in the same direction as the visitor. Jaxson hadn't heard her friend drive away. Right, she didn't have a vehicle. Brooklyn picked her up.

He didn't want to give the woman a second thought, but he couldn't help himself from stealing glimpses through the window, as they ate their watermelon. His instinct was to keep his distance. Had they gone to school together? Her and that girl had that kind of friendship. Impossible! He would have remembered her, or at least her hanging out with Brooklyn in the hallways. Maybe if he was present for all his classes, he would know.

Had he forced himself to act colder than he wanted to? Yes, and he blamed Genesis. His counselor warned him not to replace one addiction for another. He had issues to resolve, and that pretty smile wasn't going to cut it. Love had made him do horrible things, so he wouldn't allow himself to fall back into old habits. The past was behind him, and he wouldn't fall for any other traps, regardless of how beautiful they may be.

"Tomorrow night," Bryson said, pushing the grocery cart through the produce section. "Rhett made a reservation for the two of you at Lakeside Grill. It's a beautiful restaurant, used to take Collette there all the time."

"Can't." Melanie dropped her bundle of bok choy in the cart next to the onions.

"Can't or won't."

"Both." She snickered. "There's a party at Brooklyn's house tomorrow. I thought I would check it out."

"Maybe I'll come with you."

"You shouldn't."

He raised his brows, "Because?"

"It's Collette's engagement party."

Bryson tightened his grip around the grocery cart handle. "I could pop by, say hello to the rest of the family."

She gave him a wary look.

"I don't have to stick around. You need a ride, don't you?"

"I could borrow the Audi."

"Do you drive stick?"

"No," she grumbled. It had been ages since she sat behind the wheel. The transit system was far more effective in the city, especially when she smashed not one but two Mercedes-Benzes.

"What happened to your car?"

"I sold it." She avoided his eyes, pretending to be engrossed with the lettuce varieties. "Finding parking was a pain, and expensive."

Bryson glanced at her skeptically, "Why are you cheap?"

"Practical. I'm practical," she corrected.

"Practical is not having me drive you around town like your personal chauffer. Remind me to take you to the dealership on my next day off."

"It's been a while since I've driven." That was the truth, but driving around this town seemed like a piece of cake in comparison to the multi-lane chaos of Metropolis. "Don't pressure me. And I don't need your help buying a car."

"No, you'll just bat your lashes at Dad." He snickered. "Dad would do anything for his little princess."

"I am not his princess." The lettuce crunched in her fist. She wasn't planning on driving any time soon, a personal decision which she figured would save lives. And when it came to her asking for favors from Dad? Nope! No way. She wasn't a kid, she had to grow up and reject his charity.

Bryson rolled his eyes in disbelief. Melanie hated the blame she cast on him. It wasn't favoritism and she didn't ask for anyone's pity. All eyes were on her, worrying whether she wanted it or not. It looked like Dad cared more, because when they were younger she almost died, but their Dad bought him a car too.

"How was your visit? With talk of this party, did they mention me at all?" He perused through the bell peppers, deciding to pick out three individually instead of choosing the prepackaged set. "I'll bet Brooklyn misses me." As he exhaled, a short-lived smile escaped. "She must be hotter than I remember."

"Ew and ew. No and no!" Melanie stood on her toes to flick his forehead. "She's my friend and your ex's sister."

"What if I dated the wrong sister?"

Melanie covered her ears. Random guys hitting on her friend was to be expected, but her brother? She rejected the idea. "Change the subject please."

Bryson grinned. "I'm only teasing." Ugh, how did she fall for it? Brooklyn was nowhere near his type. They both had very strong personalities. Divas and know-it-alls should never mix.

"Fine, I'll tell Rhett to change his plans. Next week." He lifted a carton. "Strawberries?"

Melanie shook her head.

"I thought they were your favorite." They were, yet Melanie cringed inexplicably at the sight of them.

"They're not ripe." It wasn't Jaxson's words, but his harsh tone that the strawberries reminded her of. Something about the way the Walters' caretaker purposely acted brash with her before she had properly introduced herself, left her with a bitter aftertaste. She hadn't done anything wrong. If only he gave her the chance to make an impression and then justifiably choose to accept or dismiss her.

"They're not going to become any riper." They were a rich ruby red, large and juicy. "I'm getting them anyways." He chuckled. "By the way, it has been months. I can behave. I promise I won't embarrass you. I'll even buy you a new dress for it." He flicked out his wallet and handed her over a hundred dollars in cash. "But you have to promise to wear it to your dinner with Rhett."

"You can't buy my allegiance."

He handed her another wad of cash. "And shoes."

"Ugh, you're so much like dad, it's disgusting." Both men in their family had high tastes in fashion, only accepting designer brands. Her varsity clothes must have bugged him.

"I like to care."

"Yeah, whatever." She accepted the cash, irately. "This doesn't mean I'll fall in love with him—I'm using the both of you. Free food, free clothes, free rides. If you wanted this to work out, you already failed."

"This is why you're still single."

"Look who's talking." She sneered. "If you wanted to play the long game you should have fed her heart, not her stomach."

Bryson's fists clenched tighter. "She wasn't fat."

"I know." She poked him. "It's called a test. You failed again. You reacted. You still have feelings for her. You shouldn't go." Melanie loved Collette, but Bryson could have done a lot better than going to a restaurant. She never had thought his ex was fat. Their mom did behind his back, but their mom didn't think it was healthy for any woman to have accentuated curves. However, it stung she wasn't going to have Collette as a sister, as she was a person she could look up to and have those down to earth chats she wished she could have had with her own mother. Then there was her baking, incomparable.

"You realize there are other ways to date a girl besides taking her to dinner? I'm starting to think the failure of your relationship has more to do with your lack of romantic creativity and less to do with her current fiancé."

"I never fail. I am not a loser," he snarled. "It was her choice to let me go. It's her loss, not mine. If she wants to marry a loser, why should I care? I don't."

"Then don't, and let me hang out with my friend." Melanie took the cart from him and pushed it along. "About Jaxson. What exactly did they lock him up for?" She swallowed her breath. Never in a million years would she admit to him she spent an afternoon staring at his backside while he toiled in the hot sun. Yes, Jaxson was equal parts hot and cold. Alluring yet cruel. Her body couldn't decide between fever and shivers. "I only ask, in case… he's his brother, right? Should I be concerned?"

"Melanie, don't let either of them get to you. Jesse will play tricks on you, and Jaxson will rob you blind. Together they're double trouble. Never for one second doubt them. They make it a habit to deceive. They'll use you to get to me, don't let them. Don't even talk to him."

She smirked. "Not planning to." Technically, she wasn't lying. How could she even say hello, if Jaxson would barely acknowledge her existence?

Chapter 3

"Stop," Brooklyn commanded, smacking Jaxson's hands away from the jacket lapels. Wearing a tuxedo was a foreign concept to him. Never had he dressed this fancy for any occasion. There could have been prom, but the tickets were notoriously expensive and back then he was only interested in the after-parties.

He despised becoming a Walters puppet, especially Brooklyn's, but there was nothing he could do about it. His scratchy stubble was gone, along with his chin length hair. Brooklyn had kidnapped him for the afternoon, and when they returned, she demanded to inspect the result for a silly before-after post on her social media. Since she was his bosses' daughter, it was hard to say no.

He combed his fingers through his now straight hair and grimaced. It still had body up top, but his fingers would slip out before he could twirl the tips.

"Stop." Brooklyn swatted him again. "You look like a million bucks."

"That's the problem," he sighed, "I'm not." He stared at his reflection in the mirror, inspecting all angles of his body. The rented tuxedo fit him like a glove, not an easy feat for his thighs or biceps, considering his job relied heavily on physical labor. He was man-curvy, which often meant he would have to purchase a size up on the boxy clothes designed for men. And that was with him trying, it was easier in high school, when he and his friends could follow the trend of baggy jeans and extra large t-shirts that hung to their knees. However this engagement party was not an evening he could get away with cargo shorts and Jesse's hand-me-down shirts.

"You look like you just walked off a Bond set—Thorne, Jaxson Thorne."

"This is dumb. What's the point of an engagement party anyways?" He groaned, "And why can't I wear my suit?" His one and only suit which held sentimental value. It reminded him of family, and the loved ones, he and his older brother lost.

"Because your suit is old and cheap, and this party is more for Mom and Dad than it is about your brother marrying Collette. Honestly, I love a good transformation. Why can't you be happy? You don't have to be in the dirt all the time; you can actually enjoy nice things too, and spoil yourself once in a while."

Jaxson rolled his eyes. He lived a life for himself, indulging in his temptations, and he paid dearly for it, so lingering in the background, picking weeds out of someone else's garden was a far better alternative than the one he planted for himself.

"Thanks," he finally said. "And for the record, I'm only doing this for Jesse." A few seconds passed by, "And so I don't get fired."

Brooklyn paused from applying her lipstick to smile.

"As long as I'm around, you'll never be—brother." She picked up her phone from her makeup vanity, "Smile." Wrapping her arm around his shoulder, she snapped a few shots.

"That's enough." Jaxson slipped out of her grasp, heading out of the mansion to the backyard. Though he worked in it nearly every day, his mouth gaped.

Netted string lights hung above his head, like a blanket of stars. The outdoor pool's lights were on too, adding a lucid reflection. It looked like a wedding itself, with tables set with wide floral arrangements, dishes with silverware, and tablecloths.

"Are you wondering how much this cost too?" Jesse's voice startled him.

He turned to look up at his brother, also uncomfortable in a tuxedo.

"Probably not as much as your hair," he jested, flicking though the anti-gravity part. They both knew Jaxson looked like a pompous fool.

"Shut up." He smacked his hand away. "You must really love her to put up with all of this… fluff."

"I do." Jesse glanced over to his fiancée, laughing hysterically with one of her friends. Her golden ringlets bounced off her pale shoulders. Her smile stretched to her blue eyes, radiating the jovial energy that blended with his brother's. Her ivory halter dress was covered in a vintage rose print, which complimented her retro red lips. "Also, I'd stick to water if I were you."

Jaxson raised his brow, not surprised but curious.

"Vinegar."

"Really? Out of all the things you could've spiked it with. Don't you want her dad more relaxed this evening?"

"I thought about it, but it wouldn't be good for his medications. I don't think Collette would ever forgive me if this went sour."

"Who are you?" Jaxson teased, "What did you do to my brother? It's like you grew up."

Jesse pinched his beefy fingers, motioning only a little.

"What else should I be prepared for this evening?"

"I planted the device under their table to squeal all night—or until the batteries die."

"That thing's still going?" He bought that stupid prank toy when they were in high school together. Jaxson remembered him telling stories about the times he used it in the classroom. It would be confiscated, then he would reactivate it when it was in the principal's office.

"Unfortunately, yes," Jesse rubbed his lip, then slung his arm over Jaxson's shoulders. "Mom would be proud."

"No, she wouldn't."

"Yes she would, she would look at us and tell us how handsome we are, then wish we were half as smart as we looked."

Jaxson punched his shoulder. "You, not me. Could you imagine telling her you're marrying into a rich family? Mom would've loved Collette. I'll bet she would have always wanted a daughter-in-law like her."

Collette joined his side. He greeted her with a brief heartfelt kiss.

"You've come a long way too, and I mean it. Mom would be proud." Jesse straightened his bowtie. "Sit back and enjoy the freak show."

"You realize what her parents are doing, right?" Jaxson asked, concerned he didn't.

"You mean by planning this 'last minute?' Yeah, except they underestimate my ability to sabotage anything and everything." He smirked at his future wife, "I say, challenge accepted."

Collette nuzzled into his broad chest, By her doting gaze, she was going to say something endearing, but her jaw dropped at the sight behind Jaxson.

"What is Bryson doing here?"

Simultaneously Jaxson and Jesse clenched their fists.

"This can't be a part of my parents' plan. No. No. No. I thought we were over this." Collette panicked. Jesse grabbed both arms and held her in his embrace. He kissed the top of her curly blonde hair, soothing her. This action alone was proof they were a perfect match. There was more than friendship and attraction, they had each other. They were ready to become their own unit.

Though witnessing his brother complete someone else's life brought him joy, there was sorrow mingled with it. He should have been happy, but he couldn't change the truth. They would no longer be the troublesome Thorne brothers, they would become independent units.

"Oh no, he saw us."

Jaxson's eyes widened. Bryson Duong, the prosecuting attorney assigned to his case found him?

"Calm down, Lottie," Jesse said, perhaps to himself as well. "He's only in his car. I doubt he could recognize Jax in his new get-up."

Without a word, Jaxson darted as inconspicuously as he could around the mansion. This party was a mistake. He loved his brother, but he was not going to risk an encounter with that slippery lawyer. Every time that man appeared in his life, everything turned significantly worse. What could have been a fine became jail time. What could have been a month or two became a two-year sentence. He couldn't craft his words as clever as Bryson, but in the lost time between their last encounter, Jaxson learned silence was his best and probably only option.

He checked over his shoulder and breathed a sigh of relief. Jaxson had finally got his life together. He had a job, and the Walters provided him a small house to live in during his employment, so he hadn't had to worry about finding a place to rent. The opportunity was irreplaceable, and he knew with Bryson's dating history with Collette, Bryson would take it away from him with a snap of his fingers.

"What are you doing?" Melanie asked, as Bryson stepped out of the car. She wanted to hide her face from the disaster she expected to unfold. How many times had they gone over this? Collette was over him. It was too late to win her back.

"I'm going to say hello." He straightened his tie.

"Um, no you're not. Bad idea." She covered her mouth to whisper harshly, "You're the ex. Don't make things awkward." Her new pair of high heels clicked on the driveway pavement.

They were quite possibly the tallest pair she owned, yet Bryson still looked down on her.

"I won't." He squinted, surveying the lot.

"Don't embarrass me. I haven't made many friends yet. I don't want to be known as the girl with the stuck up—"

"I am not stuck up." With his longer strides, he was ahead of her. Whatever. He had been sulking ever since he caught wind of this event. "Are you sure you want to be here? There's still time; I could call Rhett if you change your mind." He checked his watch. "Maybe you'll have enough time to catch a movie."

Melanie lifted her hand to flick the back of his head, but he was out of reach.

Brooklyn pulled away from a crowd of young guys, startling Melanie with a much-needed side hug. "Hey girl. Cute outfit. Is it for the party, or for you-know-who?" Melanie bit back a blush, hushing her. "Aha, I knew it. He's…" She peered around the property, "He's somewhere and what the heck is your brother doing here?"

Melanie rolled her eyes. "I tried."

"Allow me. You focus on your priorities."

"I don't have a…" crush. Melanie's words faltered at Brooklyn's unconvinced grin. She patted her shoulder, then walked over to her brother in his navy suit. "Bryson! Long time, no see. Just the way it should be, huh pumpkin."

He smirked, "Don't worry, I won't be long. I just wanted to see if Jaxson Thorne showed up, so my sister would know who to avoid." Could he hint his disapproval any stronger? Like that was going to stop her from finding their gardener. Jaxson didn't seem like the corrupt person Bryson described. She refused to accept his assumptions without making her own, and she didn't need her overprotective brother interfering, considering she was already awkward around most guys.

Collette's cat walked up to her leg. Its smooth fur brushed up against her skin. "Oh look!" She picked him up, and brought him closer to her brother. "Look how cute he is. Give him a pet."

"Bah! Get that stupid cat away from me." Bryson jumped away as the cat leaped in the opposite direction.

Brooklyn gave her friend a wink and wrapped her manicured hand on Bryson's shoulder, turning him away from the direction Melanie was headed. She chased after the cat, farther into the garden. He ran under a bush, more alert in the evening than he was the last time she was at the house.

Jaxson Thorne had to be nearby. It couldn't be that hard picking out a shaggy-haired convict with rock hard muscles in a party full of rich people, but it was.

"Melanie?" her brother called out.

She wandered deeper into the garden, planning to stay as far away as possible from him until he decided to leave, whenever that would be.

Genesis waved at Jaxson when she stepped out of Ezekiel's car. Her boyfriend was quick to wrap his arm around her waist, like Jaxson had over a year ago. From the distance and her expression, she may not have recognized him cleaned up in a tuxedo. She was in a cheap denim dress and her date was in a fish printed button-up and khaki shorts.

His plan to retreat into his house and lock himself inside for the night failed. Mr. Walters spotted him and would point out his absence if he tried. Again, he pivoted on his heel, hurrying into a private nook of the property, far from the party and the roundabout driveway.

Even running made him feel uneasy. He wasn't guilty of anything recent, but it was a survival instinct to flee the scene. The soil ruined his shoes. He didn't care. He would rather scrub them for hours than face another minute with his ex. His heart pounded furiously, not from the jaunt, but the mixed emotions of the times he was happy, and the times he was robbed.

As her boyfriend found their seating arrangements, he pulled her into his arms and placed a gentle kiss on her lips, maintaining eye-contact with her afterwards—the true marksmanship of adoring love.

Rage, despair, pain, the flurry of emotions stirred in Jaxson's stomach.

Turning into the vegetable garden, he charged between the rows of raspberries, the tallest nearby shrub. It was a terrible hiding spot, but he wasn't alone. Deceived by the shadows, he thought he saw a leaning shoot. He tried to charge past it, bumping into a person.

She yelped, but he reached out and caught her in the nick of time.

"Are you alright?" he asked, as she hung on his arm. He blinked an additional time, again tricked by his eyesight. He hadn't intended to hold her in a compromising position. It was him or the uneven dirt. Thankful of his swift reflexes, all her weight was in his arms, with her stiletto-heeled feet in the air.

Her only option to return to her feet was by pulling onto his broad shoulders. He couldn't control his eyes, they wandered everywhere. From her styled brunette waves, brushing the skinny straps of her red dress covered in golden embroidery, flowers, not dragons—the pearl pendant around her neck and the matching pearls dangling from her ears.

When her chocolate eyes met his, her cheeks flushed red.

"Strange man knocking me off my feet, that's not awkward at all," she teased, probably to make light of the situation; her words paralyzed him more than her dolled-up appearance. Classy, rich, but not showy. None of the girls he hung around with wore clothes as expensive as hers.

Jaxson stepped slowly backwards, like she was a wild animal ready to pounce at any startling movement.

"Oh. I just made it more awkward, didn't I? It was a joke. I was teasing you."

Jaxson swallowed his breath.

"Melanie." She held out her hand to shake.

He stared at her open palm. Could his evening become any worse?

"Usually in this circumstance, you say your name; maybe say some excuse to why you're here." Her voice was beautiful too. She extended her hand out closer to him. "Let's try that again, I'm Melanie and you are?"

His first name had a negative connotation around town, so it was safer this way to avoid using it altogether. Best case scenario, he wouldn't introduce himself, but it was too late for that.

"Carter," he murmured, remembering how Jesse used his middle name to hit on Collette. His heart got ahead of his brain, but it was one party. Even if this guest visited the Walters again, the chances of crossing paths were slim, and slimmer if she would recognize him. He took her hand and gave it a solid shake, such soft hands. "I know why I'm in the garden, but why are you?"

"I was trying to make a sneaky escape before my friend caught me—actually that's a lie. I wanted to talk to someone." She giggled. "Okay, that's not entirely true either. See, I thought I would say hi to Collette, since I haven't seen her in ages, but then my brother tried to set me up on a date. That's beside the point." Melanie was breathing rapidly, shaking anxiously. She let out another giggle, but it turned into a squeak. She slapped her hand over her nose, bonking her nose, uncomfortably hard. "Ow."

"Are you sure you're alright?" Jaxson asked again.

She grinned wide. "I'm not usually like this."

"I'm not usually like this." Jaxson chuckled, briefly glancing at his starch white shirt. "Honestly, I had plans to ditch this popsicle stand."

"No really, I'm not actually like this." She held out her foot to show off her strappy heels. "Enjoy this while it lasts, because after tonight, these impractical shoes are going in the incinerator."

"Soap and water," Jaxson said, leading her out of the garden. "Sell them on the Buy-N-Sell instead. Or keep them." If they were designer, she could pawn them for a pretty price.

She glanced up into his eyes again, blushing. A brief memory he shared with Genesis warmed his own cheeks, and the innocent expression in her eyes made him wonder if it were safe to proceed. It was one night.

Something could happen or it wouldn't. He could wake up the next morning and forget Melanie. Wait. The name sounded familiar. Melanie. He repeated the name in his mind, matching her face in the natural lighting. She was the watermelon girl, the one in the denim shorts and palm tree tank top. The realization brought a large grin to his face, he was that forgettable.

And the grin stretched, because if he wasn't Jaxson, Carter could be whoever he wanted to be.

For one night.

Chapter 4

"A toast to Jesse and Collette, may your..." A distant relative said. Melanie and Jaxson held their glasses high from the furthest table in the back. Jaxson winked at his brother, though they hid well in the shadows.

"Don't drink that," Jaxson pinched the stem of her wineglass and spilled it onto the lawn for her, as everyone simultaneously sipped their spiked punch. Sour expressions covered their faces accompanied by vulgar shouts and rapid spits. "Here, you can have my water."

Melanie stared at Jaxson, befuddled, gulping down half the glass. Her cheeks beamed red when she spotted the lipstick residue on the rim.

He looked at the food she picked at on her plate. Two cheesecake cubes remained. She pushed the plate toward him wordlessly, and he snatched it, chomping them in one bite each.

"Hearty appetite."

"I'm a working man," he said, enjoying how obvious he laid out the clue. They had spent their entire meal together, and not once had she shown any recognition that he was indeed the man she stalked all Thursday afternoon.

"Where's Jaxson?" he heard in the distance. His eyes had instinctively searched for the source, three tables away from them. It was Genesis. She was sitting next to Collette's sister. Brooklyn lifted her head, and Jaxson lowered his.

"Mary, Joseph, Mary," he cursed.

"You said Mary twice," Melanie snickered.

"Yeah?"

"Got to love a person who respects authority. Usually when a person says that phrase it's to cover up the fact they said—"

"Yeah." He shielded his eyes from the far table. Why did Melanie have to throw that word around? Love. They just met. Admire, sure. But love was a powerful word and if she wasn't aware, her flirting with him the entire night hadn't gone unnoticed.

"Does this mean you're a godly man?"

"Far from it." He took her hand and gently led her away from the tables, through one of the hedge openings to the main floral garden. A creek ran through the property and it had its own arched bridge, one he would have to repaint next year. "When you've been through what I've been through, you either pretend He doesn't exist, or you realize you're a broken mess—big time, and He's the only one who can do anything about it. Hands and knees, even a fool like me knows heaven's help is welcome."

"It couldn't have been that bad." Crossing the bridge, her hand sliding across the rail, she bumped her shoulder into his side. "There's good in every situation. For every challenge, there's room and opportunity for growth. Whatever you went through yesterday is wisdom for today. You seem like you turned out alright." She bit her lip. "More than alright."

"You're just more attracted to me because I admitted I'm a terrible person. I'm going to ask again, are you sure you're alright?"

"What makes you terrible?"

"Oh I don't know," he sighed, about to put his hands in his pockets, but Melanie slipped her fingers into his. It brought out a soft smile and warmth to his cheeks. "Perhaps being so terrible, Dad left."

"I doubt that's the reason."

"Nope. It's the reason." He nodded energetically. "Loved Mom, hated us. Realized we were so much work, he'd rather work elsewhere and keep his money. My brother and I were terrible kids though, truly awful. If something didn't burn down at least once a week, it was a Christmas miracle. I was a picky eater. Endless energy too. Neither of us could focus in class. When we got older, we would sneak out late, go to parties, date lots of—" he cleared his throat. "We were bratty kids. Always fighting, always screaming. The only time we could get along was when we were destroying something on purpose. I liked the sounds and the messes. My brother liked the reactions. He knew how to scheme. I just did whatever I felt like."

"Okay, so it sounded like you weren't the best example for your brother, but you grew up."

"Older brother." Jaxson chuckled. "If anything, I followed in his footsteps, except he turned out better." His eyes flicked to the voices on the other side of the hedge. "Obviously."

"I suppose that's better than having a dad who insisted I become a doctor. Right field, wrong occupation. It didn't help I was forced to be held back a year academically. I caught up. When my friends were all in the classes ahead of me, it helped having a dorky brother. He tutored me, helped me bring my grades up, so I could eventually move forward. It was tough though. Growing up the way I did, we had to outperform everyone and be the best we could be. My brother thrived off it, but I just wanted to, you know… do life." Her eyes widened, "Maybe not to the extent of like burning the house down, but things like this." Melanie tightened her grip, meeting his eyes. "Have you apologized? To your mom?"

"Genuinely no, not when I should have. In my heart I have, but it's too late. There had been countless times, I robbed her, lied to her face, done all the things no son should ever do, yet she loved me all the same. Loved me through the hurt. She worked so hard to keep us alive, I honestly don't know how she did it, then cancer. Hit me so hard, instead of giving up, I gave in. I wanted to pretend the pain wasn't there, instead it cut me deeper. When she died, a part of me died with her."

Jaxson caught his eyes watering. Though he felt these emotions a thousand times before, and disclosed them with his brother and ex, the peace and acceptance from a stranger like Melanie was the warmth he had craved for years. The softness in her eyes was that reassuring hug he had yearned for.

"Sorry. I barely know you." He sniffed, miserably failing to act cool.

"Did you lose her recently?"

"Her four year death anniversary is coming up," he quaked. However her diagnosis wasn't spontaneous. He had more than enough time to pull his act together, and he didn't.

"Cancer sucks," Melanie said, "There's no nice way to put it. And it's really scary not knowing if you're going to make it. They caught mine early enough and I'm cancer-free now, but it still shook up our family. Mom and Dad took me to the facilities and treatments I needed, but I know not everyone is that lucky. I can't imagine your mother's battle. She sounds like a strong woman."

Her hand shook, and by instinct he grabbed it.

"Sorry, I just… I was really angry when Dad left for his new job. He thought it would be okay if he could buy our love, like the gifts weren't reminders of his absence. Things were never the same after I recovered. They tried to shelter me, like I was fragile." She rubbed her eyes with the back of her hands. "I don't care how many zeros are beside his name. No amount of money can improve… I'd do about anything to see him again. Time is precious."

The music behind them increased, changing to an upbeat song. He wiped his tear, then chuckled. "Perfect timing." Still holding her hand, he tugged her to the paving stones bordering the roses.

She tripped at his first dance move, but he caught her again.

"You really need to invest in better shoes." He laughed, lifting her to her feet. Her high heels were unstable on the grass versus his dress shoes. He was firmly balanced as he shook his hips. She stood still with a blank expression on her face.

"What? You don't dance?"

"I don't know."

"It's a simple yes, I do, or no, I don't."

Melanie shrugged, "Unless singing to my hairbrush counts, I haven't danced."

Jaxson belted in laughter, "You're adorable. In that case, I'll have to show you." He lowered his hands to her hips. Her body tightened at his touch, and the feeling was electric. It had been months since he laid hands on a woman, let alone in a way that made him question his current life choices. "Do you trust me?"

"Not really, no."

He raised his brows, unconvinced.

"Isn't it a sin to have your hands below my waist?"

"Yes." His grin brushed her ear, as he whispered hoarsely, "But I'm pretty certain we have already established, I am not a good person." He withheld his snicker. His touch was innocent in his terms, but her reaction, a reaction that ignited a spark within him, had only persuaded him to goad her more so.

Melanie brought out a passion he had neglected, for Jaxson was a lover, a hungry man yearning for ways to release his weighted desires. Her lips were puckered, equal parts feisty and flirty, while her eyes were coy.

This was just a dance, and if this was her reaction for a dance, it was a good call to limit this tease for one night. He would face the repercussions tomorrow, but what of it? He wouldn't have to think about Genesis ever again. His ex would have no rein on him. It was time he pushed her out of his mind and moved on, even if it meant a sampling to appeal him to a new flavor.

Jaxson stepped back, to show off his dance moves, swinging his arms, gliding into his steps, effortlessly oozing confidence. "If this wasn't a rental, I would be on the ground giving you the worm."

Melanie slapped her hands over her mouth, laughing.

"Your turn."

"Oh no." She giggled.

"Oh yes." Jaxson took a large step forward, limiting the space between them.

"Please no."

"Please, please yes," he growled, raising the stakes. Already Melanie had pushed his buttons with her soft brushes against his tuxedo jacket, lingering eye-contact, and simply how she presented herself. He was mesmerized by her and her not-so-innocent good girl act. She shook her head playfully. Still, Jaxson motioned her closer. She stepped side to side with the beat, yet with a grin, he rested his hands on her hips again.

"Relax them," he suggested.

She pouted, complying with his request.

"Relax more."

She gulped, staring into his eyes.

"Now your shoulders, waist..." His eyes travelled unintentionally to each place. He wrapped his arms around her, assisting in her rhythm, yet instead of stepping away when confident, she melded towards him. Her hands rose above her head. She was millimeters away from combing her fingers through, and ruffling up, his new hairstyle.

"This is fun," she admitted softly.

He bobbed his head to the beat, closing the distance between them, brushing up against her short dress. How did he find himself here? From giving this woman the cold shoulder, to allowing her to reignite a dying flame.

At some point, they collapsed from exhaustion. Fit or not, they could only dance to so many songs. On the grass, their bodies chilled from the moonlit sky. Hours passed and the party was long over, but the stars still shone brilliantly.

"Can this night never end?" she begged, reclined comfortably on a smooth patch between flower beds. "Can we just live our lives having days like this forever?" She pressed her back against his torso, occasionally swatting a nearby mosquito.

This woman felt perfect in his arms, but so had the others. One night—all the feels, none of the heartache.

"Carter?"

His chest tightened, jolted offbeat.

"Carter? What are you doing tomorrow?"

"Sleeping." He sat up, assisting her too. "No, wait." He yawned, "Working, then sleeping."

"Can I tell you something ridiculous?" Melanie giggled. "Tonight, I was supposed to go on a blind date with a lawyer— that's why I had to be here. Wait a second. You're not a lawyer, are you?"

"Heck no!"

"That's what I thought. You're too good looking to be a lawyer."

Jaxson grinned.

"Anyway, I thought I'd catch up with Collette, but I'm glad I didn't disturb her. It seems like she has her hands full with her fiancé. I've heard interesting things about him, but she looks happy. It's late so I'm rambling on, but coming here tonight felt like the right thing to do. Meeting you, seeing Collette with Jesse—which looks promising. Yeah, I must be crazy, I can't believe I said that."

Jaxson tapped her side. She was rambling at full speed and he was about to drift off. "You said it, but you're not wrong. They are perfect for each other."

"They are, aren't they?" she sighed, "But, I don't want to go on this blind date. Could you help me cancel next week's attempt too? I don't think I'm allowed to say no unless I have a valid excuse, and you seem like you would be a far better date."

"You don't know the guy."

"He's friends with my brother."

"True." Jaxson tsked. Dating a sibling's friend was always awkward, especially when Jesse was older by a few years. He decided to push the date comment aside. If he said no, she would be angry at him for the rest of the evening. If he said yes, he would be lying to her about the level of commitment he was willing to offer. Jaxson figured one night was all his heart could handle.

"I didn't bring my phone, but what's your number?" she asked. "I'll memorize it."

"I don't have one."

"You don't—what? Email?"

Jaxson led her to the strawberry patch, distracting her by picking a handful of fruit for her, as to give a huge, colossal hint. Asking her out on a date was out of the question, especially if lawyers were her type. He couldn't offer the stability a woman looked for in a man, if he could call himself one.

"Strawberries are my favorite."

"Yes, but..." Jaxson sighed. Did he want to admit to this perfect woman he was an ex-convict who will never be trusted by society and will probably never land a promising career because of it? In his mind he wanted to scream, "I'm not Carter!" He wasn't as strong as his brother, to hold on to a stupid scheme. His feelings already tangled with this woman, which was his problem. He wore his heart on his sleeve, and each time he paid dearly for it.

The night had to end. She needed to move on with her life and forget about him, find a man who wouldn't weigh her down, or drag him back into trouble.

Melanie chomped them down without a second thought.

"Mmm. Way better than store bought. I hope they don't mind. We're like the rudest guests ever." Her laugher caused her to squeak like a mouse, and the fragility of her small voice tempted him to hold her in his arms. "I'll tell Brooklyn later. She'll understand."

Jaxson rolled his eyes. Strawberries. The garden. Why he wore a monkey suit to this ridiculously posh party. Ding. Ding. Ding. Would she take the hints? All the signs were pointing to him, yet everything inside his resolve unwound from the slow lick over her heart-shaped lips.

"Why are you looking at me like that?" she whispered, as he stepped closer, eliminating the gap between them. "Why are… what am I supposed to… what do I…"

His pressed his lips onto hers. Nimble and cautious, her chin tucked down, but he tipped it right back up, sliding his hands into her silky hair. Roots to tips, he combed his hand through the length, sending tingles up his spine. Genesis never let him touch her hair, yet with Melanie, it was free rein. He could taste the strawberry juice off her lips, and he enjoyed it too.

He pushed the thought of his ex away with ease, pressing forward, extending each moment from her shy bashful lips.

Inexperienced. This woman had never been kissed by a man, not an earth-shattering one that spikes a fever in the soul, frying the brain to beam white. Blinded by snow, blinded by passion.

Her hands shifted from his waist, to his shoulders, with uncertainty. He smiled through the kiss, then lowered a hand to the back of her waist, pulling her towards him, taking ownership and coaching her through the process.

Immediately her hands corded around his neck, and her fingernails flicked the longest strands of his recent trim. Yeah, he was going to love this new hairstyle.

Their lips peeled apart. Jaxson hadn't felt a high like this since he could remember. How could this simple contact explode feelings of ecstasy within him? Oh yes, this woman was trouble, but he always found himself tangled in it, didn't he? Jaxson pressed his forehead against hers, gasping for breath, yet she leaned toward him with puckered lips, wordlessly begging for an encore.

The night was late. Jaxson pulled her into his shoulder, and held her in an embrace. His heart beat rapidly against her chest. His broken heart that lay shattered in a million pieces, melted in this fire, and forged into a new shape. Love wasn't meant to be sudden, but as he held her in his arms, he knew he wasn't going to let this one night go.

Then he remembered, to her he was Carter, and love based on a lie wasn't love at all.

Chapter 5

"Melanie?" Brooklyn gasped, both hands covering her mouth. She was in her pajamas and the screen on the phone in her hand glowed against her cheek.

Melanie blushed with guilt, wishing to bury her face into Carter's chest, but he vanished. In a blink, he leaped over the flower bush, climbed the stone walls, and with long-legged strides, he booked it into the shadows.

"Bryson has been freaking out. He's sent me like five hundred texts asking where you've been. Why haven't you been answering your phone?" Brooklyn reached out and wiped a smear of lipstick off the side of her cheek, "Was that—"

"Carter, yeah." Melanie pulled her hair to the side and fondled the ends, reminiscing on the recent memory of his large hands brushing through them, and the tingly sensation it gave her at the scalp.

Strawberries and cheesecake. Never, not once had she been kissed so delightfully.

"Carter, huh?" Brooklyn bit her lip, momentarily glancing in the direction he ran off to. The man could run. Maybe he was a police officer. With his build and physique it would make sense.

"Please don't tell Bryson. Please, please, please," she begged. If it weren't for her heels and this small dress, she would fall on her knees and grip her friend's ankles.

Brooklyn crossed her fingers. "I'd rather not." She nibbled on her lip. "Now that I think about it, he's kind of perfect for you."

"He is, isn't he?" Melanie sighed, turning to the direction he ran off to, then pouted her sore lips. "What am I saying? How could I fall for a guy that quickly?" She rested her hand over her chest. Her heart drummed happily against her palm just by thinking about the mysterious man. "I don't know how this happened. I mean just the other day I was crushing on Jaxson hard—oh don't tell Bryson that either. His looks! I mean, I was obviously crushing on him for being like ridiculously hot, but so is Carter. Why is this so awkward? It wasn't like a real crush anyway. I didn't quite get the best look at his face with the sunglasses and the sun was like in my eyes and… he was really broody too."

"They look alike, don't they?" Brooklyn bit her lip.

"Kind of, not really. Jaxson's hair was longer and I doubt he even knows how to tie a tie, or if he owns a shirt." She laughed louder than she intended. "I've seen a lot of guys in suits, but Carter was something else." She kissed her pinched fingers three times. "Tasty." Melanie pouted the moment she realized he hadn't just left the party, he had left her. "Aw, how am I supposed to find him?"

Brooklyn snickered, "Believe me, you'll see him again. You could say he's here like all the time."

"He is?"

"Yeah, he practically lives here. Next time you come over, we'll find him."

"We will? Are you sure?"

"Oh yeah, he's like family to me."

Melanie grabbed her friend's hands excitedly, "Oh thank you. Thank you!"

"Someone slept in." Collette snickered at Jaxson the following afternoon. He spent what little of his morning he had left picking up remnants of trash and décor left after Jesse's coworkers packed up their rental supplies. He had been too tired to shower before bed and too sluggish to clean himself up before lunch. His hair flung out in misguided wings, a suiting representation to how he felt inside—the sober equivalent to hung-over.

Leaving his place in a pair of shorts and a t-shirt was an accomplishment.

"It's too bad we didn't get to see you, you know, at the party," Jesse teased, sitting comfortably next to his fiancée with his arm resting over the back of the couch. His dark curly hair had been growing back, but it was nowhere near the shaggy length it was when Jaxson was in jail.

"First, I don't work Sundays," Jaxson said to Collette, though today he had. He crossed his arms at Jesse, "Second, I was there. I promise. The whole time and I behaved."

"Define 'behaved.'" Brooklyn stepped in, bringing a bowl of fresh picked strawberries to the coffee table. Looking at them, they reminded him of Melanie, her taste, and how divine she had been in his arms. Before chomping on the fruit, she rubbed it against her lips, painted them bright red, then twisted them upward in a wicked smile. "…Carter."

Jesse and Collette snickered. They all knew. They had to.

"Oh c'mon. It was one night." He smeared his palm down his face, "It was just a kiss."

"Anyways," Collette opened her spiral notebook and clicked open her pen, "we can talk about this later, whatever 'this' is. We have a wedding to plan, so let's make it quick before Mom and Dad…"

On cue, her parents entered the room, taking a seat on the adjacent couch.

Jesse lowered his beefy tattooed arm to take her hand, stroking it for comfort. Her young cat meandered by, jumped onto her lap, and curled into place, purring.

"When are you going to take that stupid cat?" Jaxson hissed, "All it does is poop in my flowerbeds."

Jesse laughed, "Soon." He checked on Collette and beamed wide. "We're going to elope, and we want you and Brook to be our signers."

"Witnesses," Collette corrected.

"No." Collette's mother blurted, "We cancelled Venice for this wedding. You're our daughter and we want you to have the wedding you deserve. No shortcuts."

"This is not a shortcut, and we didn't ask you to cancel your trip. We thought this through," Collette insisted, but her mother's scowl increased.

"We're paying for the wedding, and we are having a ceremony."

Jaxson averted his gaze from the regularly steamed carpets to the abstract paintings on the walls, like other items in the room. The large canvases of paint splotches had cost the Walters a pretty penny. He was certain he mimicked the same thing on the kitchen wallpaper when he was five.

Jesse's brows furrowed. Rarely did he visibly show irritation. "What Collette is trying to say is," he clasped tightly to her hand. "We come from two very different families. Yours being well… big and well off, and ours, being Jax and I." Jesse took a deep breath and exhaled slowly. "We appreciate that you're offering to foot the bill, but Collette and I want this to be simple. My parents won't be there, and it will be emotional enough as is."

Jesse didn't have to track their dad down; it would have been a fruitless excursion.

"Please Mom," Collette insisted. "You had your wedding thirty-ish years ago, let me have mine."

Her mother crossed her arms. "You're right. Weddings are a family affair and I birthed you; therefore, I am going to be there. It's going to be in a church. You're going to have a reception, and photographer. There's going to be a cake, and you're going to be beautiful in your white dress. You will have a ceremony and we will pay for it, or you don't have it at all."

Jaxson kept his distance, but it seemed clear to him, they agreed to not have a ceremony, so her mother's threat seemed a tad redundant.

"It doesn't have to be simple," her mother insisted, "Jesse will be too distracted by your beauty to think about other things. He loves you so much."

"Mom!"

"Don't Mom me, missy. You dreamed of this back when you were dating Bryson. Just because Jesse can't afford it, doesn't mean you can't have it. We agreed to cover the costs. You're going to have the wedding you want. You will look back on it for years. Years!"

Jesse gritted his teeth and Jaxson's jaw cricked. They would never forget their own mother. They needed the time and space to process her absence on the special day.

"One month," Collette said. Mid-August was when their mother passed. "I can't live in this environment for any longer. He is my fiancé. He is going to be my husband. Why can't you see him for who he is?"

"The man who put vinegar in our drinks?" her father snarled, eyeing Jesse up and down.

"Harmless prank," Jesse said nonchalantly.

"Harmless? That was five dollars a head for those drinks—non-alcoholic, literally down the drain. And we do care. We hired his brother. Without us, he would be robbing banks all over again. Why can't you be grateful?"

"It wasn't a bank," Jaxson interrupted. He had been guilty of vandalism, destruction of property, theft of other things, but he wasn't caught for any of those crimes.

"You still robbed someone of their livelihood."

"It was one ring and I served my time."

"You served a third of your time. We bailed you out. You're supposed to be on our side. Don't you want to see your brother standing at an altar?"

"I want what he wants." Jaxson decided not to go into specifics of his case. He shouldn't have had such a lengthy sentence, but it was that vile lawyer Bryson Duong who multiplied his sentence to absurd proportions.

Jesse rolled his eyes and puffed out a heavy breath, "Fine. We'll have a ceremony. I'll wear a suit. I'll do all the stupid traditions, whatever, as long as it's Collette I'm marrying. It's one day."

Jaxson snuffed out a quick laugh. One day. Yeah, the whole 'one day' mentality got him in a mess alright. He was a strong man, then he saw Melanie, and his guard went down. One dance. One kiss. Yet all he could think about is how he can have one more.

"Count me in," Jaxson said, turning for the door.

"Where are you going?" Jesse asked, following him to the foyer. Far from the family meeting, he lowered his voice, "Are you going to meet up with your new girlfriend? Who is it by the way?"

"Jesse?" Collette called out.

"I'll be a minute." He followed Jaxson out the door and sighed with relief. "I love her, but hate them." His words were stronger than the truth. Obviously Jesse tolerated them, and enjoyed finding ways to bug them, which was different than hate, but he clued in to his brother's frustration. The Walters expected him to be someone he wasn't.

"Jax?" Jesse said, pulling him out of his stupor, "What happened? I thought you'd sworn off girls and dating altogether."

"I thought so too." Jaxson rubbed the back of his neck and overlooked the yard, specifically to the area beyond the hedges where they had danced. There would be an extremely slim chance he wouldn't have those songs stuck in his head all week. His cheeks warmed, thinking about her smile. "She's a good girl. Too good for me. She won't remember, and that's fine."

Jesse grabbed his arm. "Now hold up. She won't remember, why?"

"She thinks I'm a rich dude named Carter. The moment she sees me for who I am and for what I can't offer, it's game over. She'll move on quickly. You don't get it."

"I get it."

"No, you don't," Jaxson snarled. He pressed his lips together, immediately regretting his hasty response. "You had years of friendship for Collette to look back at when she forgave you. Melanie doesn't know me, and what people think of me is worse. I'd rather pretend to be Carter than have her know the truth. The worst you had to fear was being annoying. There's more at stake here. I'm not ready for this. It's too sudden to have any weight. What if I still have feelings for Genesis? What am I going to do if she dumps your coworker?"

"What if she dumps Zeke?" She wasn't going to dump him, or at least, he wasn't going to be the one to end the relationship with her.

Jaxson shrugged. He shared a lot of good memories with Genesis before his incarceration. If they could go back to the way things were—they couldn't.

"Jax, just promise me, whether you find love again or leave it as is, that you won't relapse. If you like her, give it a shot. Don't be like me and chicken out. Don't wait years when she's right there in front of you, and for the love of all things good, don't push people away."

He reflected on the season before Jesse became a delivery truck driver for Price Event Rentals, how after their mother's death, he let himself and his hair grow. Jaxson didn't understand at the time, but as Jesse visited him later in jail, he could see his decline with each visit. He had subconsciously made himself repulsive, yet Collette had sparked something in him, made him care, and it gave him great joy she brought the best out of him. Jaxson missed the man bun. Not many guys could pull it off, but his brother could. The direction of this subject matter was dark, so he pointed him to his detached accommodation.

"I'm thinking about saving up for a motorcycle."

"Wouldn't a car be a better investment? You can't ride a bike in the winter."

Mr. Walters peeked at them through the window, hinting they would need to return.

"Yeah, but I want a motorcycle."

Jesse scowled. "Jax. I understand it's exciting to have money in your pocket now, but long-term, you can't garden forever. You can't buy the cool things all the time. It sucks, but you go down that path, you'll…"

Jaxson lifted his hand. "I'm not going to steal, anything, ever. You have my word. I was only thinking about it." Brooklyn was generous enough to lend him her car whenever. If he needed a truck, he had Jesse's. When it came to vehicles, he had his bases covered.

"Just like you were thinking about buying a gaming computer last week, or how you wanted whatever tool it was. Get a car."

"But…"

"Get a car, trust me." Jesse combed his fingers through his short curls. "I'm trying my best, I really am, but what happens if their charity runs out? You can't be going for impulse buys or impulse dreams. I'm proud you're saving up since I know how difficult that is for you, but be smart. If you're desperate, you could always stay with me, but there could be that one day. You can't live off of the system, if anyone knows it would be us. Please, plan ahead."

Jaxson rolled his eyes. Plan ahead? He had planned to pop the question and settle long before Jesse. If he learned anything from his time locked up, it was that life threw curveballs, and he needed to adapt. Stocks fail, basements flood, and houses burn down. At some point, Jaxson would have to live his life. Even if it's a night of strawberry kisses.

"They'll fire me any chance they get. I know. In fact, if anyone knows what they're saying behind our backs it's me. Don't worry about me. You just deal with your own problems." Jaxson nudged him to return inside. The father-in-law was waiting.

Chapter 6

Melanie paced back and forth in her bedroom, in those same stupid strappy heels she wore to Collette's engagement party. They accented her outfit perfectly, but wearing them was a gamble. On one hand—or foot, they were a hazard to her wellbeing, and the other, they painfully reminded her of the man who literally swept her off her feet.

The man who never called, never said anything to Brooklyn, never attempted to revisit the magical moment they had the weekend before. Similar to the Cinderella fairytale, the clock struck midnight and the magic disappeared. Melanie was back to her boring life.

In the dragged out parts of her day, especially filling out patient reports, images of him and his enchanting smile would encourage her to push through with her mundane tasks. She wondered how it was, that some days she could forget forever, but there were other moments that flittered through her subconscious on repeat.

Like the moment his eyes were spellbound on hers and he eliminated the remaining space between them. How his fingers combed through her hair, tickling her scalp, tantalizing her nerves. How her skin chilled and fevered from his daring touch. The texture rough, yet his love tender. How she let him kiss her and how her heart awakened, begging for more.

"Ready?" Bryson asked, not in a suit, but still presentable as if he was going on a date himself. "Did you call Brook? Maybe she will want to come along."

"Yeah and no." Melanie stuck out her tongue, trying to avoid her freshly applied lipstick. It was a rosier color, complimenting the pale foundation. The joke was old and still as gross as the first time he brought it up. "She's busy planning her sister's bachelorette party, which I will also be going to." During the call, Melanie repeated her evening plans multiple times in the slight chance Brooklyn would consider passing the information onto Carter. Because a friend who knows she is totally shipping for a guy wouldn't let her date a different guy.

Unless they were Brooklyn, who viewed everyday life like her reality TV show and thrived off the drama.

"I'll be in the car." Bryson closed the door, leaving her alone in the apartment.

Melanie stood in front of the full-length mirror in her room, catching her reflection. She looked like a doll in her puffy short sleeves and frilly skirt. She kept her hair straight, pinning her bangs up with a large, ribbon bow hairclip.

"Here goes nothing," she sighed, slinging her purse over her shoulder, and following her brother into his black Audi. They cancelled the dinner date idea for a local music concert. Eating with a stranger alone could have been insufferable, but she loved music, more now she had danced to it. What if Carter was the type of guy who regularly went to concerts? She insisted Bryson tag along so she wouldn't mistakenly find the wrong Rhett. The description he gave about his friend was pathetic.

Blond and blue eyes—how was that supposed to help? That could have been half the town.

When they were inside the theatre, Melanie gripped her brother's arm. One step inside, and the air conditioners stunned her with the needed icy blast. She thought about slipping on a pair of tights or leggings underneath her dress earlier, but with the late summer heat, she wouldn't have been able to bear any additional layers.

"Personal space." He slid her hand off. She grappled him again. He rolled his eyes and sighed. "Rhett's a good guy, I swear. It will be fun."

Their mother said the same thing about the doctor and their dinner date seemed more like a study date comparing notes. To her, good and fun weren't words she put together when describing a lawyer—her brother being the exception—sometimes.

Nothing could top her evening with Carter. She would forever put that man on a pedestal, and yet, he not once made any effort to contact her. What reason would he have to distance himself? Was it his past? She already informed him it didn't matter. In her books, a changed man was better than a good man who compromised.

She longed for a love that could be real, and the man who stood before her, a giant, was anything but. Yes, she wasn't supposed to judge by appearances only, and yes any man could wear ridiculously overpriced branded clothing to a first date, but the wristwatch never lied.

Poor men didn't wear gold watches. If they own them, they kept them locked in a safe, but Rhett wore his like it was just another in his collection. He was big money, probably bigger money than her family, the kind of money which meant, if a relationship would occur between them, she would have to keep face, inflate egos, and choose his friends over hers. Sure, she was thinking too far ahead, but would her years in nursing school be for moot?

Then again, Carter seemed well off, with his expertly styled hair and well-fitted tuxedo. He never wore a gold watch, but he had mentioned living a life pleasing for himself. Perhaps he leaned on his career during his hardest times as the distraction he needed away from his sick mother and hard home life. Many successes work their way from the bottom to the top. To Melanie, rich wasn't bad, it was the money mindset. She didn't want her life governed by dollar bills, and one look at Rhett was enough.

Not that being a lawyer was easy, as she observed living with her brother. But she doubted Rhett would ever empathize with her past like Carter had, or if he could be a person she could open up to about it.

It was important for her to be acknowledged for her feats, not as the cancer girl or her daddy's money. Melanie wasn't sure which one would be worse, so she often hid both massive elements of her background from the friends she would meet.

Until Carter.

It just seemed right, like he needed to hear her story, like she needed his.

Tonight Melanie was simply meeting her brother's friend. Nothing about it had to be romantic. She could keep it platonic, sit through the concert then go home. Yes, be polite. She could plaster on a pretty smile and pray they would never cross paths again.

They scooted to an available trio of seats in the middle, near the front row of the crowded theatre. The band had yet to arrive, but their display and instruments were set up, under a warm yellow glow of stage lights. Behind it was a row of pallets threaded with LED lights, and vibrant blankets tied on with ropes for splashes of color.

"Hey." Rhett reclined in his seat, soaking her in with his chilling blue eyes. Pale eyes were beautiful and definitely on her list for the perfect man, but the slicked-back hair was an absolute travesty. His overgrown bangs looked like they had been cemented into his skull with the amount of gel used. Melanie wondered if she poked it, if it would make a crunch sound.

"Hi," she said sheepishly, adjusting the skirt of her dress to sit down. She pressed her knees together, tugging the hem for it to cover her thighs. She wanted to show some leg, not all of it. Maxi dresses were never her thing, yet there she was, a petite girl cursed with long legs. The heels didn't help.

"Hot day, huh," Rhett said to break the awkward silence.

"Yeah." Melanie's gaze fell to her toes. "Why the…" she motioned to his hairstyle, "it's very business professional," and not concert casual, she wanted to add but held her tongue graciously. What was she thinking, rudely pointing out his hair? Who was the hypocrite now?

He chuckled, "I don't like hair in my face. My hair. Yours, well…" he glanced over to Bryson texting on his phone.

"Oh shoot," Bryson said, standing abruptly.

Don't you dare! She wordlessly warned her brother.

"I have to get back to the office. Don't have too much fun." He winked at Rhett, then excused himself elegantly as the lights dimmed and the performers entered the stage.

"Yes!" Rhett groaned with relief. "Bryson's cool and all, but nothing kills the mood more than a third wheel, especially an older brother."

Was Melanie supposed to smile? Bryson was more than an older brother; he was her best friend when she had none. He had been there by her side during the chemo treatments and afterwards when she had to return to the real world. He could have hung out with older guy friends like any other brother, but he chose to replace the negative memories for unforgettable ones, spending the prime of his teen years with her. Plus she thought that was super rude for him to say about the person she lived with. She looked to the main singer instead.

"He wasn't kidding when he said you were pretty. I mean, a brother would never admit their sister is—" he cussed when he could have used any other adjective in the English language, "hot, but…" again the vulgar words slipped off his tongue so casually.

Melanie politely pointed to the stage, strongly hinting she was going to focus on the evening's performance.

"Not much of a conversationalist, huh? That's okay, being a lawyer," he flaunted the job title like it was a pick-up line, "I'm basically a professional sweet-talker. Your brother and I go hand-in-hand. He's all business," Rhett lowered his voice, dipping to her ear, "and I'm all play."

"Well, you heard the man, not too much fun," she teased lightly, while searching the dimmed room.

No Carter.

"Do you always listen to what your brother says?"

Melanie gulped, trapped in the situation. Bryson's apartment was all the way across town and again, she had to wear the ridiculous heels. She should've listened to Carter and sold them immediately.

"Family is important to me and he's kind of my roommate." What else could she say? "If you don't mind," she finished her sentence by motioning to the band. The speakers increased in volume as the melody transitioned from background instrumentals to an exciting song. She stood with the crowd, eventually pushing away his initial comments, and allowed the music to sway her.

She bounced to the beat, not fully dancing, though if it were Carter, she wouldn't have hesitated.

Rhett's hip brushed against hers. A chill shivered down her spine, opposite of the fever from Carter.

Ugh, enough of this comparison. It was toxic, and ruining her date. She could've said nicer things, asked questions showing a genuine interest in him, instead of ignoring him for the music. Carter moved on.

He was an amazing kisser. Whatever. He was a fun memory, not a keepsake.

Rhett bumped her again, this time partially behind her. The shock of his touch threw her off balance, and she fell forward, sliding metal chairs, and smashing her face on one in the process of catching herself. She tapped her nose, swelling, but in place.

Sniffling, she could sense an oncoming trickle of blood.

Rhett reached out for her, but she pushed him away, snatching her purse, and hobbling through the row, bumping into nearly each body she tried to avoid. What a klutz. *Stupid heels.*

Melanie rushed to the bathroom and cooled her face, then pinched the bridge of her nose over the sink. Her shoe was broken and her dolled up face was covered in sweat. Her armpits weren't any better.

After a few minutes, she stepped out, refreshed, but with a sick feeling in her stomach. Her intuition prompted her to leave, yet her morals held her back. It would be rude. *We all say things we don't mean,* she reminded herself.

Rhett stood before her in the foyer, "Are you okay?"

No.

"Yeah," she whispered, quiet as a mouse.

"They're almost over. You want to come over to my place, relax a bit?" The offer was gentlemanly. His gaze was not. If the eyes were the portal to the mind, and the mind reflected the schemes of the heart, the heart a gateway to the soul, she wanted none of it. It was dark. Those icy glacial eyes spoke volumes as they grazed her body, disintegrating her outfit in a brief once over.

"No, thank you. I have work in the morning." Nope, that was a lie. It ate at her conscience. "Not the morning. It's a late shift, but I have things to do beforehand." Something surely, she could figure it out the next day.

"You don't have to stay the night."

Her eyebrows shot up. "I wasn't planning to."

Rhett rubbed his lips and laughed. "It was a joke." It didn't seem like one. "Say, Bryson wasn't kidding, you're as sweet as they get. Pretty and smart. If you weren't shy, I wouldn't be this lucky." He flashed his million-dollar, perfectly straight, bleached white teeth.

Melanie wasn't shy. If anything, she was really awkward. Falling into Carter's arms, nearly breaking her nose on a blind date, she may have been a bundle of nerves, but she wasn't shy. She chose to not accept every guy who asked her out, especially creeps like him. She bit back the words, though she had a strong urge to blurt, "And that's why you're single." Was he blind to her obvious signals? Her body had turned down all his advances. They were looking for two very different types of intimate relationships.

Stepping towards her, he flicked the bow on her head. A few pinned hairs slid out in front of her eyes. Melanie scrambled for her phone in her purse. She needed a ride and she needed one quick.

Seconds later she heard ringing from the door behind her. The sign read, "Staff Only." Was his device confiscated?

"What?" Bryson asked. His voiced muffled from the other side. He sounded out of breath, like he went to the gym. It made more sense then returning to the office during a weekend evening.

"Are you busy?"

Rhett pinched his lips, holding back a snicker.

"The concert isn't over yet," Bryson said matter of fact.

Melanie knocked on the door.

A woman they passed in the lineup answered, short of breath, flushed, and displaying a deceptive grin as she pushed past them. Bryson's cheeks burned red, shuffling with his shirt buttons in one hand and his phone in the other.

"Not a word," he growled to Rhett.

Melanie gasped at her older brother's indecency. When their eyes met, shame filled his face. He was supposed to be the golden child. Why was he philandering with a stranger? Her heart sank. She looked up to him, especially when she needed the push during college. He was sweet, patient, ethical.

Not tonight. No wonder Collette dumped him.

"Not from you either." At the final shirt button closure, he grabbed his sister's wrist, and dragged her to the car. Under the twilight sky, the muted summer heat hit them instantaneously.

"You deserve to be alone." She sneered once buckled, refusing to look him in the eye. "How could you stoop so low?" He knew right from wrong. He was the protective brother. This wasn't the Bryson Duong she grew up with. Where did that guy go?

"She was interested."

"Interested in what? Who are you and what have you done to my brother? You're weak." What happened to his justice complex? His respect for women?

"Do you want to walk?" he asked, hitting the brakes harder than necessary at the red light. "Do you want my help or not?"

"I never asked you to set me up."

"I never asked for your opinion." His fingers curled around the steering wheel, as he proceeded in traffic. "Why do you have to be difficult? Why do you have to challenge everything?" he snarled. "His hair? You honestly mean to tell me you have a problem with his hair?"

"And his watch."

"You're unbelievable," he growled.

"Likewise." I lifted my nose in the air. "If I wanted to date your snobby friends, I would have already. He isn't my taste."

"Oh, you have taste now?"

Yeah, but she wasn't going to tell him who, or why it gave her a sudden hankering for a slice of cheesecake.

Chapter 7

It had been another long week for Jaxson, grooming the property for yet another party. It seemed each weekend would bring out another full-blown festival. Otherwise their house was quiet and empty. Collette Walters was subject to wearing a plastic crown with a cheap tulle veil. Her cousin climbed out of the pool squealing as they ran across the lawn, chasing after her. He never dared to trespass indoors, but the old self would have been tempted.

If Jaxson had a mansion like the Walters, he would have everyone living with him—friends, family, and definitely that hot girl Melanie. She would have a room down the hall, but he'd sneak into her room, purely for the thrill of being secretive. The two would tiptoe outside silently to the pool and enjoy a midnight swim. They'd tread close, kissing with their heads above the water. She would peter out, but he would continue on, holding her in his arms, cradling her under the stars.

He would have a room with a pool table, a private theater, and he would order pizza for delivery, and could cover the extra cost. Yeah, he'd have to kiss her in that theatre too. With the lights dimmed. It would start with an innocent hand on her knee, but with the screen reflecting into her eyes, one look, and he would be a goner.

He sighed, pausing from his latest drawing. He was in the middle of inking his current graphic novel. The coloring would have to wait until the next day when he had better lighting.

Ironically, landscaping for the Walters turned him away from the appeal of big money, when he could observe the life from an inside perspective. Collette's father seemed to work all hours of the day, popping in and out for meetings or appointments. Colleagues would stop by, often knocking on Jaxson's door asking for his whereabouts. Mrs. Walters' situation wasn't any better. Working here, volunteering there, and shopping everywhere. He never complained though. Honestly, he wasn't certain what she did with her day, but it was none of his business. Wasn't money supposed to buy free time? They were the busiest couple he had met, too busy to watch the flowers they paid him to care for bloom.

Observing or preparing parties he was never invited to, or belonged, stung. The younger Jaxson would have panted like a dog, sitting adjacent to a lively bachelorette party. If it wasn't meant for his sister-in-law, or his current disposition on love, he would have definitely considered crashing it.

The old Jaxson would have impressed at least one of them with a cannonball entrance.

He laughed at another shriek, Collette's, probably from one of Brooklyn's filthy jokes.

As much as Melanie loved her friend Brooklyn, watching the women who could have been her sisters, squeal about another man was a terrible idea. Bryson blew it, yeah, and she had given him the cold shoulder all week. Kissing random girls wasn't like him. He was a mega dork, but she supposed people did change over time. Bryson was less of a bookworm and had become more pretentious in recent years. Yes, there were women who were attracted to that; if shallow were what he wanted.

Was her brother that lonely that he dropped his morals for readily available affection? She refused to believe this was a permanent change for him, that he still longed to deeply care for someone like he had her. If only he would deal with his own baggage instead of shoving it onto her.

Though she wanted to set him up, she wasn't that cruel. Melanie shivered, remembering her horrible ambushed date last weekend, and how Rhett had stared at her.

The ladies giggled over the gifts, whispering promiscuous comments to each other. Melanie couldn't stomach another second. Normally, she had a stomach of steel, she had to as a nurse; however, the moment her emotions pooled into the mix, she was in trouble. Melanie tugged on Brooklyn's sleeve.

"I'm going to go inside. Socialled out."

Brooklyn smirked. "You're staying for our sleepover though, right?"

"Of course." The bachelorette party seemed like a good idea at first. All girls, no creepy guys, and maybe catching a glimpse of the hot gardener. Since Carter was a ghost, she wasn't opposed to another game of I-spy-the-man-candy.

Except she felt like an idiot when she arrived. Why would the gardener be out this late anyway? The bugs would eat him alive. Lucky bugs.

Entering the Walters' home, she headed towards the baby grand piano in the room off from the foyer. She lifted the lid, and slid her fingers over the ivory keys. It brought her to her childhood. Her parents had doubled her lessons, so she could play at a level where she could accompany Bryson on the violin. They were a few years apart, yet musically, they were like twins.

She sighed, feeling lost. It seemed like these days she never knew the man at all.

Enough staring. She positioned herself to play, and out came calming melody after melody. First it was a classical piece, then she transposed the rendition, for jazz, then pop—not just any pop song, one she and Carter had danced to.

It was like she could hear his raspy voice singing along to the words. He was one of a kind. His voice had depth and grit. There was no superstar quality to it, but it weakened her knees.

No wait, she could. He was too young for there to have a mature grit, but his voice, the way it sounded, just like she remembered, gave her goosebumps. She whipped her head around, and there he stood.

"Whoa! You really are like a brother to... Are you her brother?" she asked Carter.

"Almost." He grinned. It was briefly endearing. In a holey t-shirt and threading shorts, he slid on the bench beside her, placing his closed sketchbook on the stand. "I was wondering who it was, since it's usually Collette, but she is outside." He smirked. "My turn."

Though his skill wasn't quite to her level, it was soft and serene. She caught herself humming to the tune; recognizing the song, she finally sang out the lyrics. He turned to her, smiling, still playing, admiring her voice. The wordless praise brought heat to her cheeks.

"Our neighbor was a piano teacher. We couldn't afford the lessons, but Mrs. Millar used to let me play. She was an old lady and we used to stay at her house if Mom was working late."

"I assume you spent a lot of time there."

"When I was a kid, yeah."

"What now?" she asked. "Are we going to sneak off and hang out all evening again?"

He grinned, not opposed to the idea. "Naughty, naughty."

Melanie bit her lip, "Perhaps not all night, until the party is over. I promised Brooklyn a sleepover. We have girl matters to discuss."

"Girl matters, like what? Like the boy you kissed in the strawberry patch?"

"I wouldn't call him a boy, he seemed much more like a man." She brushed her fingers along his bicep, causing him to fumble through the notes. "What I don't understand, is how he wouldn't call me the next day. You might not have a phone, but Brooklyn here does. Everyone on this planet has one except you it seems. You could have borrowed…"

"I could have done a lot of things, and trespassing shouldn't have been one of them," he glinted with zero regret. A flame flickered in those blue-grey eyes. "Curiosity got the best of me, and if it weren't the cat, you will be the death of me."

At the mention of the cat, Damien Junior brushed up against their legs. He was under a year old and ridiculously affectionate.

"You have a problem with cats?"

"Just this one." He grinned, picking him up and petting his skull. "Thinks he can poop in my flowerbeds."

Collette's cat nuzzled his stomach then curled himself in his lap.

"Your flower—" Melanie bit her lip. Her eyes widened as she soaked in a better view of the man beside her. He had a five o'clock shadow, and the same rich chocolate hair, only it was shorter. There was a smaller tattoo on the far arm she hadn't focused in on, and he was less polished than their previous encounter. "Jaxson."

Her brother would be furious, but then, he had secrets of his own. So what, Melanie kissed a criminal. She liked it too! Why should it matter who she chose, if he locked lips with strangers. She didn't need his approval, just like she didn't need her daddy's money. Melanie was going to take her chances too.

"Jaxson Carter, yeah. I lied to you. You hate me now?"

"Why would I hate you?" she laughed, taking his hands off the keys. "I mean, I've heard things about you, but I doubt they're true. They don't match up with the man before me."

Jaxson crooked an eyebrow in disbelief.

"Is it true you went to jail?"

He nodded.

"Because you robbed a bunch of diamonds from a jewelry store?"

He rolled his eyes, "Technically yes, but I only stole one thing… and I regret it."

"But is it ever one time? I'm not accusing you or anything, but do you ever feel like stealing more?" She looked around the Walters' home. There were paintings, ridiculously large vases, and electronics sprawled over various surfaces. The place was a gold mine for a thief.

"Maybe we should take this conversation elsewhere." He led her outside to the small detached house, where he stayed. "Make yourself at home." He kicked off his shoes at the door, and crashed on the couch in the living area.

The walls were white and the furniture seemed brand new, following the latest trend. The only hints of color were from the woven threads on the large rug, and on the wall were pressed flowers in small picture frames in a square group of nine, each one with a unique blossom. It was far different than the sloppy and stinky bachelor pad she expected.

"You didn't answer my question." Melanie's eyes narrowed. "Are you going to steal again?"

"That's a loaded question, don't you think?" Jaxson opened the fridge and cracked open a soda, offering one to her, but she refused. "Feeling like doing something and doing it are two different things, and quite frankly, I don't know the future. I hope I'm strong enough to never give in." He gulped a full sip from the can, gasping at the end. "Then again, I gave in to you, so there goes my resolve."

"How am I the enemy here?"

"You're not, but you're trouble. I can sense it."

"Do I make you feel hostile?" she asked, picking up a throw pillow and hugging it in her arms. It was obvious the space had been decorated by the Walters, and Jaxson owned very little of what was inside.

"It was one night," he growled. Melanie couldn't determine to whom, so she decided to poke the bear. If he shared the same feelings, which she thought he had, she could shut her brother up once and for all with his date suggestions.

"About that, since we aren't officially dating, I went to a concert the other night—on a date."

Jaxson's eyes bugged out.

"With that lawyer guy I was telling you about."

His jaw cricked.

"It was fun. We danced together too." If dancing together meant standing beside each other in their row. "He couldn't keep his eyes off me."

"I'll bet," Jaxson hissed through his gritted teeth.

"This doesn't bother you?"

"Why?" He grinned wickedly, seeing through her scheme. Placing the can down on the coffee table, and holding a steady gaze on her, he slowly crawled toward her, breaking her resolve.

"Yes," she whispered, not like he had said anything, but she answered the question herself, "It bothered me like the whole time, he was all like…" she mimicked Rhett flicking her gaze up and down his body.

"So he was attracted to you? Shocker." Jaxson pulled the pillow out of her grasp, "What are you afraid of? Haven't I already torn down your walls?"

"Apparently I haven't removed yours."

"Nothing you could do could—"

She yanked the collar of his t-shirt and pulled him to her lips, not feeling guilty of tearing the fabric worse than it already had been. His cold and rigid act fell apart, and he melted instantly.

"Not fair."

"Life isn't fair, but you knew that already." Her eyes danced with danger. "And I was right; it wasn't just one night to you either, was it?"

Jaxson stood, clutching his nearly empty soda, wishing momentarily it were spiked with something stronger. That was a dirty trick she played, and it wasn't the first time a girl had toyed with him. Genesis charmed him out of most of his paychecks. Melanie followed him to the counter and wrapped her arms around his torso from behind.

"I corrupted you," he admitted, hating how perfect she felt this close, how complicated it would be to give her the world he wanted to offer. Jesse's warning flashed through his mind. After their rushed wedding, it wouldn't be long before he would be out of work, and what girl would be attracted to a homeless criminal? He would be a dead weight she would eventually sever off. It was best he cut ties sooner than later.

She squeezed him again.

What was one more night?

"This is the part where you ask me out, for real," she said softly. She was too short for her lips to meet his ears.

"Is that so?" He freed an arm to finish off his drink. "What if I don't, so you can keep dating that lawyer?"

She pretended to gag.

"I'm not interested in him one bit. At all! I hope I don't ever have to see him ever again. The guy can't take a hint."

"Most guys can't." Jaxson chuckled, turning around. He couldn't avoid her a second longer. In a black crop top and sunflower skirt, she was a sight to behold. "I can't," he mumbled, forgetting what she was referring to.

"Then don't resist."

"You don't know what you're asking for. You forget I'm a terrible person." Twirling his fingers in her soft hair, he added, "You're too good for me."

"There is no such thing as too good."

Raising his eyebrows, he took one look at her, and shook his head. "I beg to differ."

She bit back her lip and her cheeks flushed a soft rose, matching her lips.

"Please. Give me some way of contacting you. I have to tell my brother something the next time he tries to pair me up with another one of his lawyer pals."

Jaxson shrugged, realizing teasing her was more effective on her than it was him. The thought she could make him jealous put a smile on his lips. He wasn't looking for love, and it would make his life a million times easier if she just moved on without him.

"Just say no."

"But it's not that easy, I already hinted that."

"Don't hint it. Say it."

"But…"

Jaxson gripped her thigh, like it were a training exercise. "Say it." He purposely crossed the line to test her resolve. His thumb dug into the muscle. She was too polite and it concerned him.

Her lips parted.

"We can't read your mind. You have to say it."

She swallowed.

"Remember, we've never been on a date. I have rudely kissed you and I will again. I'll obsess about you day and night, and those thoughts will be far from pure. Tell me to stop." Why was she silent? He was a stranger. It wasn't long ago that she called him by the wrong name.

"Perhaps, you're a little more forward than me."

He pinned his free arm above her head until all she would see was him. "Tell me to stop."

"Maybe you should tell yourself to stop."

"This is for you."

"And maybe I want you."

His chest heaved up and down, his face flushed and damp with sweat, he grimaced. This beautiful woman didn't fear him. She wouldn't hate him, and for every push, she pulled.

"You can't let a guy walk all over you, Mel. You have to say no. You have to be rude and up front, or he won't get it. So say it."

"I want to get to know you more, Jaxson. If you think I'm going to give up on you, you're wrong. I'm going to visit you often. In between shifts, I'm going to harass you with my own charms, so it's only fair, and I'll keep doing so, because in my heart, we are dating. I won't stop you from falling in love and you can't stop me."

"Then do this for us." He slipped his hand into her long wavy hair and tugged on it, tilting her chin up for another kiss, "Tell me to stop, before I can't."

"I will… after you kiss me."

Chapter 8

Jaxson rode the lawn mower with one hand draped on the steering wheel and had a sloppy grin on his face. He finished the first set of diagonals and was working on the opposite angle for an artistic diamond pattern. Weeds were to a minimum, and the flowers were in full bloom. The vegetable garden was abundant with fresh produce. With a bucket full of ripened cucumbers and more on the way; he would have enough to pickle. Brooklyn promised to help, she claimed it was for social media, but ever since she stopped flirting with him, their friendship grew exponentially.

The rose colored glasses were in full effect. Life was perfect. The sunshine burned against his bare back. Trails of sweat dripped down his spine, yet everything in his life was looking up. He had an amazing job, with the freedom to sing and shout as loud as he wanted. He could goof off and as long as he finished his tasks, he could flirt with Melanie the whole time.

Unfortunately she was at her own job for most of it, but ever since the bachelorette party, she made an effort to visit him every day between her shifts. Another reason he tolerated Brooklyn, if he was genuinely busy, Melanie could walk inside and hang out with her best friend.

He loved every second of it, peeking over his shoulder to catch her peering through the sheer curtains. Sometimes for the thrill of it, he would flex his muscles or complete the task in a full body motion that was purely for her entertainment, even if it slowed him down.

Hours later, Jaxson was still riding on the high of their last kiss before she had to dart off to work, when Collette and Jesse ran out to the lawn calling for him. He removed his ear protection, turned off the engine, and slung them over the seat as he hopped off.

"Everyone is here now," Collette said, hand in hand with his brother.

"Everyone for?" Jaxson looked around the empty backyard.

"Inside. Today was the only day we could arrange everyone in the wedding party to meet before the rehearsal, so we're going to go over a few details, but since you're the best man, we are definitely going to need you there."

"Best man?" Jaxson inspected himself covered in grass blades and speckles of dirt. "Let me change first."

"No time. Stella has to go to work soon. Grant was of course late." She groaned.

Jesse rubbed her back, "It's going to be okay."

"Yeah, but Mom and Dad want this to be—"

"It's going to be okay," Jesse repeated, as Jaxson rushed over to the cast iron bench he draped his shirt on earlier, and slipped it over his head.

Inside, Jaxson planted his feet and lost his voice instantaneously. The wedding party wasn't massive, but right there in front of him was the one couple he had tried to ignore all summer.

Ezekiel locked eyes on him and protectively wrapped his arm around Genesis' shoulder. One look at her and the wind was knocked out of his chest, for the wrong reason.

Why would this bother him? He had moved on. He was with Melanie now. Looking at her, he felt a taste of the sweet love they once had, but when he glanced away, all what was left was the hurt and the hate. Bitter. Why would it matter that the woman he used to kiss was now kissing this other guy?

Collette's hand shook, her nerves getting the best of her as she offered the tray of fresh fruit around the room. Some were from the garden, but if he had his appetite, he would have been more drawn to the meat and cheese platter on the table between the sofas.

"Sit. You're being weird," Brooklyn whispered to Jaxson, patting the seat beside her, but Collette took it, preoccupied with everything else going on. With nowhere else left to sit, he took the vacant spot beside Genesis, widening the gap as much as humanly possible between them.

"Do you want something to drink?" Genesis asked.

"No." Jaxson avoided her eyes. Anytime he looked into them, he was a goner, one of the subtle admirable traits about her, they way she could seduce a man with her gaze. It wasn't fair to Melanie. She worked so hard to break him after he pushed her away. She was too good for him, and he didn't want to let that go, but he disappointed Genesis. He was bound to hurt Melanie too.

"Okay?"

Collette waved for everyone's attention. She spent the first few minutes explaining the venue, the photography session, and then she looked around the room. "So we've paired you up for the procession. Brook and Jax, since you're maid of honor and best man, that's a given. Zeke and Genesis, and that leaves Grant with Stella."

Grant and Stella stared at each other from opposite sides of the room. Grant was a beefy giant who proudly wore his plaid flannel shirt and a ball cap that had probably been through World War I and II with the beating it had taken. With his mud speckled jeans, he must have driven there straight from the family ranch. Then there was Stella. She was a fragile twig with her long hair tied into a side braid, in a cotton maxi dress. Jaxson knew not to put labels on people, but it wouldn't be a long shot to guess she was vegetarian or vegan too.

They glared at each other with feigned grins, clearly repulsed by each other. Was Jesse pulling a joke on his best friend, or was Stella actually a close friend of Collette's? Grant retained eye-contact, chewing piece after piece of pepperoni. She had to lower the plum she was about to bite into, like she couldn't stomach his laid-back mannerisms.

"Any questions?" Collette asked.

Grant and Stella shot right up.

Genesis nudged Jaxson. "Can I speak to you for a moment, in the kitchen?"

"No."

"Jaxson," she hissed. He rolled his eyes, then followed her, not taking a seat at the bar stool beside her, worried he would ruin the Walters' upholstered barstools. "You can't ignore me forever, okay. Don't act like I can read into your game. Believe it or not, I know you like really well. It's almost like we used to date or something," she said dripping with sarcasm. "I'm sorry at how I ended things, I can't say it enough, but Jesse is important to the both of us, and we can't have your glum attitude ruining his big day."

"If it weren't for me, you would have never met." Jaxson clenched his fists. "This could have been us. Don't you get it, Genny?" He immediately regretted shortening her name like that, it was often a tag he used when he teased her, particularly during their dates.

"What do you want, Jax?" she hissed. "Do you want me to break up with Zeke? You know why I ended things."

"Yeah, because you thought I couldn't take care of myself. Look at me now! Proved you wrong, now didn't I? You gave up on me, thinking I'd always be trapped in the system, falling in and out. It was never about love with you. It was about what was convenient, and Ezekiel was right there." Genesis opened her mouth, but Jaxson turned away, "I hope you're happy, because I am way, like a freaking million times, better without you."

"Jaxson," she caught his wrist and softened her voice. Looking over his shoulder to Zeke distracted in a conversation with Jesse, she whispered, "I get it, you're no longer a bad guy, but should things go back to the way they were—minus you know that?"

He swallowed hard, weighing his options. The good memories outweighed the bad. People did change, they could turn back from their horrid mistakes, but did he want to revisit the past? He had loved her, but was this old love worth returning to? As he let her proposition sink into his head, he overheard Grant's shouting.

"I work the field. You eat it!"

"It looks like all those injected hormones have truly altered your brain," Stella muttered in response.

"Injected hormones? You eat fake meat; if anything is injected, it's your over-processed so-called health food. At our ranch, if we don't grow it, we don't eat it, and my oh my, if it ain't doused in a healthy serving of barbeque sauce, it ain't worth beans."

"Stop it! Stop!" Collette called out. "There will be both meat dishes and vegetarian options available at the reception. Can you pretend to get along, at least for one day? For me?"

They both crossed their arms and looked away in opposite directions.

Jaxson pulled his arm free from Genesis. "We had something good, but you could have someone better. For Jesse, I won't be a jerk and neither should you." His gaze flicked to Ezekiel again. "That man loves you." He decided not to mention Melanie. Though she was his world, they had only known each other for less than a month. He didn't want to jinx it.

Chapter 9

"Guess who." Small hands covered Jaxson's eyes as he was hunched over a flowerbed. She hung off his shoulders, and as he stood up, she tipped sideways. Spinning quickly, he caught Melanie in his arms, and leaned down to kiss her, tipping her towards the flowers.

She squealed more the lower he dipped her.

"Don't want to get your shirt dirty?" He chuckled heartily. She kissed him gently on the lips, admiring the warm rich sound of his laughter.

Her chocolate eyes darted wide open when a bee zipped past them. She dug her nails into his skin, holding on for security.

"Don't worry, they won't hurt you." He propped her up. "As long as you don't get in their way, you'll be safe. They're more afraid of you than you are of them."

"Yeah, but they could still sting me." Her eyes squinted from the bright sunlight behind him.

"They could, but they won't." He flicked his sweaty ball cap off his head and slapped it on hers. "At the worst they may confuse you for a flower, I would."

Melanie's cheeks flushed red. "Stop. I can't afford to blush. It's already outrageously hot out here." She took the hat off and fanned herself with it. "You should take a break. It is not safe to be outside in the heat of the day. I saw the weather report. It's only going to get hotter for the next week." She turned to the mansion. "It might rain on their wedding day, though I wouldn't call it a bad omen. We need it."

"I'm fine."

"Have you been drinking water?"

"Yes. Today was iced tea, but I needed a treat."

Melanie crossed her arms. It wasn't like he hadn't been out gardening every other day in this sunshine. She had nothing to worry about. His body could handle the heat. What he couldn't handle was how adorable his girlfriend was when she doted on him.

"Don't. I'll be fine."

"You should cover up, when it gets bad like this."

"It's already warm enough." Adding layers would only make him sweat worse and double his laundry pile. No thanks. "Besides, you like it," he teased. Jaxson always caught her gawking when he was at work. And she called herself modest. As if. Did he care? Not one bit.

"That's not the point." Melanie licked her lips. "Are you wearing sunscreen?"

"Yes."

She pursed her lips, then jumped as another bee buzzed by. "Bah! They're everywhere."

Jaxson laughed, "Well you are in a flower garden and you are wearing yellow. They're just doing their job. Maybe later, I could show you their hive… if you're brave enough."

Melanie jumped again. "Maybe I should change my shirt. I'm stealing yours." She picked up the blue shirt hanging off the pear tree and sniffed it. "…or not."

"Why don't you borrow one of Brooklyn's?"

Melanie fluttered her lashes.

"If you think I can read your mind, I can't." He laughed.

"I want one of your shirts to wear, so I will be reminded of you wherever I go."

Jaxson stabbed his spade into the soil, "The closet is all yours, although I may warn you, there's nothing worthwhile in there." Before jail, he was underweight and flat broke. During his sentence, he beefed up with not much else to do but draw comics and work out. His brother's clothes weren't worth borrowing, so he relied heavily on the limited selection provided by the thrift store. Considering his job was what it was, why would he go fancy? Plus his shoplifting days were over, so it was break the bank or wear rags.

She giggled then ran straight to his house. As he watched her skip around the flowerbeds, it made him realize, he hadn't given her anything special since they'd started dating. He couldn't afford fancy dinners out, so they ate in. He never dressed up, even if she had, because they were chilling at his house. He hadn't done anything exceptionally special for her yet.

She deserved a little something.

Jaxson picked up his hand shears then snipped at a few stems. With a handful of blossoms, he rinsed out his iced tea bottle and shoved them inside. Call it an eclectic vase, it did the job.

"These are snapdragons," he said to himself, practicing his speech. "They were my mother's favorite. I used to call them popcorn flowers." He snipped a few more. "And these, though they don't look like it, are actually a part of the rose family. They're real hardy. Mom had a bush by our driveway growing up. They used to always be the first ones on the block to bloom, but that's because Jesse and I used to pee in the neighbors' gardens." He shook his head. "Nope, too far."

He heard a vehicle pull into the driveway. Familiar with the engine sounds of the Walters' vehicles, this peculiar one piqued his interest. By the time he reached the side of the mansion to check out the car, the guest was already at the door, obstructed from view by fully bloomed flower bushes.

Jaxson whistled at the black Audi. It was a beautiful car and made him think about his oncoming paycheck. He was so close to owning a vehicle, he could taste it.

"Brooklyn, hey." Why did that voice sound familiar? Jaxson scooted to get a clear view, with the flowers in one hand, and the shears in the other. Squatting next to a flower bed, looking busy, he glanced up to that lawyer that sent him off.

Bryson Duong leaned against the threshold in navy slacks and a white buttoned shirt. His expensive watch flashed in the sun. His black hair was shorter, like it had recently been cut and his face was smooth, free of any shaving cuts.

"What have you been up to this summer?" His eyes scanned her tank top and shorts outfit briefly, then looked away like he had better places to be.

"Oh you know." Brooklyn crossed her arms, subtly glancing over her shoulder to Jaxson, then back to Bryson. "Being a bridesmaid and all—the maid of honor."

"Did you get my text?"

"Yeah."

"And?"

"That's kind of weird, isn't it? You had a serious relationship with my sister."

"What if it was the wrong sister?" Bryson shifted, rolling up his shirt sleeves. "Brooklyn. You're obviously the hot one, admit it. I'm this, you're that. You wanted it to end. It's over. No strings. You and me, one night out. Help me forget her, okay? Let's forget the past. Didn't you want a turn?"

Jaxson clenched his fist. That was his future sister-in-law the lawyer was harassing. No one messed around with his family.

"Bryson?" She squinted, inspecting him head to toe as if there was something off with his health. "Even if that were true, I already have a boyfriend."

"But Melanie said you were…"

"Jax! There you are." Melanie rushed over and leaped onto him in a hug. Her arms and legs wrapped around his body, like she was a lemur and he was the tree. It knocked the flowers out of his grip. The bottle popped out and rolled down the driveway, as the flowers lay flat on the pavement.

"The flowers are for—" he paused, admiring her in his shirt. She had tied a knot so it wouldn't cover her denim shorts like a frumpy dress. Yet there was something off-putting about her appearance. She had thick dark hair that was naturally straight, narrow eyes, and a natural golden sheen to her skin. Her ethnicity never concerned Jaxson, but those features, it was the exact same as that guy.

"Melanie! What the—" Bryson cussed, storming towards them, spitting out other vulgar terms en route.

Jaxson stepped back, covering his mouth not to gag. He had a string of curses he was about to spew himself.

"Get your hands off my sister. This is sexual harassment. You sick piece of—"

"Bryson stop," Melanie pleaded, pushing Bryson away. He was steaming red. "It's not harassment, he's my boyfriend."

Jaxson interjected, "He's your brother?" Both his and Bryson's eyes shot up to Brooklyn. "You knew and you didn't say anything?"

"You're too cute together, how could I?"

Jaxson stepped back, "I can't." He shook his head. "I just can't," he repeated, walking hastily to his house. The doorknob rattled after he locked it. Melanie rushed to the nearest window, tapping it. "No." He fought the dam of tears. How could life be so cruel to him? He had turned his life around. Did it mean nothing? Was he cursed to suffer heartache?

"I'm not my brother," she shouted.

True, but her brother was not a person to tick off, and he flipped him off unknowingly with this romantic fantasy.

"Is your last name Yang or not?" As he said it out loud he felt foolish. It was obviously fake. "Don't answer."

"Jaxson!" Bryson growled from the door. "I'm only going to say this once. You stay away from my sister, and I'll behave. That's more than a fair deal. Don't you dare try to send your people. Mine will lock them all up."

His people. Jaxson rolled his eyes. He had to cut ties with those people long ago. They weren't his friends. Yes, many of his few true friends were criminals, but like them they had cleaned their lives up or were trying. He wasn't going to mess around with pushers and enablers.

"Bryson, stop," Melanie pleaded. "You don't understand. I love him. He's not the same. He's good now."

"Shut up and get in the car."

A minute later, Jaxson stepped out of his house and watched the Audi drive away, trampling the fresh petals under his summer tires.

"How could you!" Inside their apartment, Melanie kicked Bryson in the shin.

"How could I, what? Protect you?" He tossed his keys on the counter and turned on the air conditioner. "Jaxson Thorne is a cold-blooded criminal. You think this is about love? He is only using you to get to me."

"Ugh! You couldn't be any more wrong. This has nothing to do with you, Bryson. If you didn't scare him off, maybe you could see how harmless he truly is."

"Harmless?" he cackled, "That's rich." He reached over to the fridge and grabbed himself a beer. He tossed one at her. She caught it, but placed it on the end table beside her. "Drink. You're going to need to, if you want to make it through this conversation."

"I don't need booze to process this crap show. You think I can't handle stress? I work in the flipping Emergency Room."

"For less than thirty days. Drink." He chugged half of his in the first gulp.

"No."

"Whatever. Suit yourself, but don't say I didn't warn you."

"Warn me about what?"

"Jaxson Thorne has sticky fingers, Mel. Before his failed jewelry heist, he had a habit of pick-pocketing tourists and shoplifting in stores. The guy couldn't hold a job—fired for being late, absent, absent-minded, or stealing from the business itself."

"In the past, but he's different now."

"They always are." He rolled his eyes. "You stick to healing sick people, and leave justice to me. That's so you, Mel. Looking for the good in the worst of people. Some people need to suffer."

"But he's suffered enough."

"He will never suffer enough. Guys like him will never learn. They were trouble as kids, they flunk out of school, engage in petty crime, next thing you know, they're bashing their pregnant girlfriend's head against the wall. You can lie to yourself all you want, but guys like him don't change, not for the long haul. One slip-up, and they're back to the monsters they were born to be."

Melanie broke down in tears. "You don't know him."

"I know everything about him."

"No." She shook her head and repeated herself, "You don't know him like I do." She wiped her tears with the back of her hand. "He's hurt, deeply hurt, lonely and afraid. He's trying really hard to fit in, but everyone is pushing him out."

"Or he's toying with you. Melanie, no offense, but you're an easy target."

Furious, she kicked his shin again. "He is my boyfriend."

"No. You're going to end this now, or I'm going to tell Mom and Dad. I understand you have feelings for him, but they will go away. Pick someone else, anyone else, just no criminals, okay? Promise me no criminals. I swear, Mel, if you go back to him, I will take legal action."

"You can't do this to us." She reached out to shove him into the cupboards, but he caught her wrists.

"I can and I will." Squeezing them until they stung, he snarled, "Watch me."

Afraid, she retreated to her bedroom and locked the door. Pulling out her phone she dialed Brooklyn immediately. Her body shook as she waited for her friend to pick up.

"Yeah?"

"Brooklyn, please do me a favor." She sobbed, scrounging around her room for a tissue to clean up her face. "Check on Jaxson for me. Check that he's okay."

Collette stormed into the yard, holding her phone in the air. She looked around vehemently, as if she were going to chuck her device onto the ground and smash it.

Jaxson paused from his work. "Is everything alright?" Clearly it wasn't.

"Yes. No." She pocked her phone into her shorts. "Wow it's hot out here. Can't be out here too long or I'll turn into a strip of bacon."

Jaxson nodded. A sunburn would not be pleasant for the wedding photos. He and his brother were a darker white than the Walters, and weeks in the sun had turned him into a more golden shade than Melanie, though she liked to stay out of the sun as much as possible.

"Sorry. I'm just in panic mode. The wedding is in less than two weeks, and all the reception venues are booked up." She scrunched her nose. "We might just have to have it here."

"You have the space."

"Yeah, but not the parking."

"So, people will walk a little bit. It worked for the engagement party."

"This is true." She let out a relieving smile. "But that was only part of the yard. You would have to have the entire property in tip top condition." Her eyes trailed over to the bridge, then shifted to a few of the rickety benches between flowerbeds. "You already work really hard around here, are you sure?"

"Collette, you're family."

She wrapped him in a tight squeeze.

"Whoa, Jax. You're really warm."

"Yeah." He pointed to the sky. It was only morning, but it would probably be the hottest day of the summer according to the weather report. "I'm good, but uh… what if it rains?"

Collette grinned. "I'll take care of it. We have plenty of tents. I'll reserve the largest one, but could you set up the bouquets the night before? Your mom used to garden, right? Maybe we could surprise Jesse with some of her favorites. Do you remember what they were?" Her thoughtfulness brought warmth to his heart, but his thoughts scattered off when her phone buzzed. "Got to take this," she said, rushing inside the house. "Ugh! This heat!"

Jaxson had spent the next morning repairing and sanding the decorative arch bridge. He leveled the benches, reinforcing them too. There were many things to love about his work. One being he had work, which was a blessing in itself. Two, he could play in the dirt, make a mess, and shift from task to task. And thirdly, he could see the literal fruit of his hard work. It was tasks like these that helped him feel accomplished. He grinned remembering how as a youngster, the shenanigans he put others through when he used tools without permission, often hurting someone—usually himself—or something in the process. This would be by accident of course. What once was used for destruction, he used for repair.

To him, tools were toys, and with a property like the Walters', he had an entire arsenal at his disposal. The sun may have been blazing, but amidst the strenuous labor, it was playtime.

With Mr. Walters' permission, he would level out and add stone to various dirt paths between the various gardens, but first he needed to paint.

With zero cloud cover, he figured he wouldn't need to wait an entire day for the second coat. The sun would dry up the first layer in no time. Jaxson twisted the lid of his iced tea and squirted it into his mouth. After a while, his saliva was thick, and drinking water became bland, so on the hot days like this one, he switched it up. Besides, he needed the sugar and caffeine boost to propel him through the overtime.

"Jaxson," Brooklyn called out. She wore a large brim straw hat and a palm leaf print romper. "Maybe you should take a break."

"I will," he hollered back, after I'm done painting.

"Jaxson," she said with more severity in her tone, "did you have lunch?"

He went to shake his head, but he had an oncoming headache. "No. I wasn't hungry." He had a granola bar and banana in the morning, but once the afternoon sun came, his appetite had vanished.

"Hey," she placed her hand on his shoulder, "I know you're hurting, okay? Melanie called again."

He had been ignoring her, because he loved her and like his ex, he knew that if he isolated himself, the sharp pain would eventually become a dull ache. However, Melanie was different. He wasn't sure how to cope, so distracting himself with work was his best option. Why should he be surprised she lied to him about who she was, if he did the same? Would he have kissed her if he knew what her brother could do to him? The fact he hadn't added more stress. It was like a ticking time bomb, only the clock timer was missing. If Bryson didn't hate him, he hated the likes of him, so there would be no winning her family over.

It wasn't fair of him to have her choose between him and her family, even if her brother had no soul. *Her brother had to be my prosecutor.*

"Take a break. Talk to her." Brooklyn offered her phone. "Maybe your stomach will stop bothering you once you figure this out."

"It's complicated." He brushed another streak of white paint on the bench arm.

"You should listen to her," the woman beside her said. He recognized the voice immediately and turned to his mother, astonished by her presence. She sat cross-legged in the grass, in a corduroy skort and horizontal striped t-shirt. She had her trusty tan visor, the one she wore often when she worked in her small flowerbed.

Was he high? He checked the paint can. It advertized to have lower fumes, he paid extra for it, plus he was working in an open space with the best possible ventilation. Jaxson chose to ignore the voice, remembering the other times she had visited.

She would often tell him to go grab something to eat, or join him in song. He was loud, but he didn't care, because his mother was by his side. It would be late at night, probably two or three in the morning, he would be walking down the orange line, skipping in his step. She would shove him when he tried to do something wild, and he'd fall flat on his face on the pavement. It wouldn't hurt though. He would just laugh, and lay there for a while.

But there Mom was in her go-to gardening outfit. He swallowed, but his stomach tightened at the taste of its acid creeping up his throat.

Brooklyn stepped in front of him and his project. The sun beat down on his back.

"Move," he whispered.

"No." Brooklyn crossed her arms.

"Move!" he said with more urgency. Dropping the paint brush, he vomited into the hydrangea bush. Too weak to return to his feet, he collapsed, lying on his back.

"Jaxson?" Brooklyn rushed over to him, placing a hand on his forehead. His eyes fluttered open and shut, to her screaming, then again, when she sprayed him with the water hose. She smacked his cheek. "Jaxson!" She lifted her finger above his face, prompting him to follow the movements. By her panicked expression, he must have failed.

Opening his eyes again, he was in the passenger seat of Brooklyn's car. She reached over and buckled him in. Another blink, Jesse was assisting her, carrying Jaxson inside the local hospital.

"Hold on to this," Jesse commanded, shoving a bag of frozen fries, holding it against his torso.

He blinked into consciousness. "This is overkill. I'll pop a Tylenol and have a nap."

"No. It's too late for that." His brother furrowed his brows, engraving the severity onto him. It wasn't the first time Jesse dragged his sorry derriere to the emergency room, but this time it came as a shock to the both of them.

The nurse opened the door. "Jaxson?" she called out. She had long platinum blonde hair and bubblegum pink scrubs.

Jaxson followed her inside walking slowly, his surroundings spinning around him. Jesse stood close behind, ready to catch him at a moment's notice.

"Sit down, we'll run a quick urine test, then someone will come and ask you questions in a moment."

Jaxson crashed onto the metal folding chair. The nurse took his vitals. Her eyes widened at his temperature.

She gave him a clear cup with an orange lid. When he returned, the blonde nurse prompted him to an available bed, sliding the curtain shut.

"See?" Jaxson pushed himself to smirk. This wasn't his first rodeo. He understood their protocol and each second here was a second lost back on the estate. The nurses would move back and forth from patient to patient, dealing with real emergencies first, him not being one of them.

"Just let them do their jobs," Jesse prompted. "No need to be a smart aleck, alright? This is serious, so stop pretending it isn't." He picked at his eyes, acting tough, but Jaxson's episode seemed to spook him.

"I saw Mom." Jaxson sighed. "She was in the garden with me, and I didn't listen to her."

"Jaxson, don't look too deep into it. You were hallucinating."

"Yeah," he sighed, closing his eyes, resting the thawing food over his forehead.

"Drink some water," a nurse interrupted, holding out a paper cup with a straw poking out. "There's ice in it." His eyes were still deceiving him, since the nurse in burgundy scrubs had an uncanny resemblance to Melanie. Her hair was tied up in a bun, held up with a handful of bobby pins and a rubberized headband.

She cracked icepacks against her knee and placed one on his stomach and another under his knees.

Another nurse stepped through the curtain, pushing a cart.

"I'm here to run a few blood tests."

While she was setting up the vials, the other nurse ran him through the generic questions. His name, date of birth, and if he had allergies.

"Have you consumed any alcohol?"

"No."

"Do you smoke?"

"No."

"Are you on any prescription or recreational medication?"

He paused, glancing over to his brother. "No."

After the second nurse took her samples, the first one tied a rubber strap around his upper arm, tapped his wrist, then inserted an intravenous port.

"You're dehydrated. Just sit back, we're going to pump up your fluids, okay?" She stepped out for less than a minute, returning with a saline bag, and hung it on the IV stand. Jaxson handed his cup off to Jesse then drifted back to sleep.

When he woke, the nurse was sitting in Jesse's seat with her clipboard in her hand.

"He went for a walk to clear his head. The doctor will come in shortly."

"Quiet day?"

"It's eight, and yes. But before he comes in, I'll need to ask a few more questions… now that your brother is out of the room."

"Shoot." He tried to sit up, but his body felt weak. The nurse adjusted the bed for him to an upright position.

"Have you consumed any alcohol?"

"No."

"Smoker?"

"A few puffs like ten years ago," he chuckled. "Haven't we already gone through these questions?"

"It's important you're truthful with me so we can give you the treatment you need." She raised her brows, in disbelief. "Have you consumed any alcohol?"

"Sober for a year." He counted the months on his fingers, "Fifteen months."

"And drugs?"

Jaxson bit his lip. "My blood will be clean." But she wasn't referring to his blood test. It was his previous medical history. If the doctor was to prescribe him medication, he would have to be honest. "Not recently."

"When was the last time?"

He rubbed his eyes. He wasn't deceived. It was Melanie. It shouldn't have surprised him, he knew she was a nurse, but this isn't how he pictured himself visiting her at work. He imagined her working with babies in the maternity ward.

"I won't take it personally, patient confidentiality. This is for you, not me."

As if! This information would completely destroy her image of him. He left his past in the past, but he doubted a good girl like her could simply glance over it. Jaxson reached for her hand; holding on, he caressed her palm with his thumb.

"Let me help you. Could you be specific?"

Chapter 10

Jaxson ran both hands down his face.

Melanie wanted to skip past the question more than he did. She didn't want to admit her brother could have a valid point, but why wouldn't he? That's what made him such a powerful lawyer, he always had an argument, and he would get in their face and push his opponent until he won.

"I sobered up in jail, no relapses."

"Which drugs, Jaxson?"

"Codeine." He licked his lips. "Heroin, and sometimes cocaine."

She peeked at the inside of his arms, but he covered them immediately. Why hadn't she seen the signs before? Because she wasn't looking? Bryson was right. She always forced herself to look at the good, blinding herself to the bad. Melanie reached over to inspect the injection sites. Small, bruised dots remained.

"It's in the past."

Melanie closed her eyes, taking a deep breath. Still her heart sank. All it would take is one relapse, and the good man she fell in love with would return to the monster her brother imprisoned. After those hard drugs, it was a miracle the man was still alive.

"I know it's wrong, and I haven't, and I will never go back to it again. Today has nothing to do with that. Back then, I wasn't myself. I was in a lot of pain. I missed my mom. I used to believe I could see her when I'd shoot up, but it was all a deadly lie. Please. Trust me." He gripped her hand, pleading. "At first it was to numb the pain. I already struggled with focusing; when Mom got sick, I couldn't function. I wanted clarity. I wanted to shut my brain up and escape. I promised I'd stop, but I couldn't. Then she died, and that's when I got into the hard stuff." He breathed heavily. "I tried to keep it a secret from my ex, but she eventually found out. I used less, but…"

"You spiraled out of control?"

Jaxson nodded in tears. Melanie picked up the tissue box and offered it to him. He ripped two tissues out. "It's in the past, but sobriety isn't easy either."

She sat down, grabbing both his hands, and hushed him.

This was not the place to reprimand him. Whether it was a year or ten years, he fought the battle each and every day. He didn't have to tell her, she did the math in her head. The shock of jail sobered him up for good. She tried to hold back a grin, forcing her lips together to hide her expression. Her brother was wrong, he was a changed man.

"I'm proud of you."

His jaw dropped.

"I'm surprised and blessed. You could be here for those reasons today, but you're not. The doctor is going to come in and tell you that you suffered from heat stroke. He is going to recommend you take it easy for the next few days and book an appointment with your family doctor. This could have been fatal. The heat could have fried your heart or kidneys—regardless of your medical history. Jaxson," her eyes watered, yet a smile worked her lips, "this time it would have been the sun that could have melted your brain."

Jaxson tugged her closer, by the hem of her scrub top. Her lips neared his, but she pulled away.

"Not now."

"Such a good girl," he teased.

"When Bryson lets up, I'll pop over." She tapped his hand, playfully chastising him. "Behave. No sunshine. No more iced tea."

"You're killing me."

"No." She beamed. "You're slowly killing yourself."

"Mr. Thorne?" Mr. Walters knocked on the door of the caretaker's home. Jaxson smirked at himself. 'Mr. Thorne' seemed foreign and unfitting for a miscreant like him. Climbing off the couch, he approached the door.

"Yeah, boss?" Over a week had passed since his hospital visit. The days remained hot, but he forced himself to limit his workload to the bare minimum during his recovery time, and do it in the evenings after the sun had set.

Mr. Walters glanced out to his groomed property. Jesse had dropped by in the evenings after work, to help Jaxson catch up, but the lawns would need to be mowed one last time before the big day.

"I heard you were interested in buying a car." He shoved his hands into his pockets, and jingled the spare change. "I've bought a few, enjoy doing so, and I'm good friends with the owner at the Chevrolet dealership."

Jaxson laughed. "No offense sir, but I don't have dealership kind of money."

"I know." He grinned. "Which is why you and I are going to bargain him into one steal of a deal. I'll help you out."

Jaxson's eyes widened in surprise. "You will?"

"Yes. First, your work here hasn't gone unnoticed. You didn't have to work yourself to death to appease me. If just one of my employees were like you, I could sleep far easier at night."

"Second, it will make for a great story at the office. Let's talk him down at least ten grand."

Ten grand exceeded Jaxson's budget.

"Our receptionist is retiring soon, if you want a job that's less physically demanding, I could put in a good word to the manager."

Jaxson scratched the back of his neck, "Thanks, but no thanks. I can't do math. Reading hurts my brain. I'm not a phone guy." What other excuses could he come up with? He grimaced, eventually he would have to pick out a smartphone and plan that suited him. "I flunked like all my classes in high school."

He slipped on his baseball cap and sunglasses and stepped into the heat. Following Melanie's orders, he was wearing a loose dove grey button up shirt, and brought with him a frozen water bottle, that would thaw in the sun at the speed and convenience to whenever he needed a sip.

Mr. Walters escorted him to his car. He flicked on his own pair of sunglasses then led them down the road.

"I never had a son, and this weekend I'm going to gain two. Legally one, yes, but this is something I've always wanted to do."

"Do what?" Jaxson asked, distracted by the passing vehicles, the news report on the radio, and the icy blast of air conditioning blowing on his skin.

"I wanted to buy cars with someone who knows and actually cares about them. Thanks for changing the oil, by the way."

"No problem."

"What model were you thinking?"

"I wanted a Harley, because why not?" He smirked. "Jesse talked some sense into me. I probably shouldn't be borrowing people's cars anymore, especially if I'm the type of guy to be accused of stealing one. And as sexy as it would be to have Mel riding there with her arms around me, I don't think she would be a fan."

"What you're saying is you don't want to borrow my daughter's car to take her friend out on a date?"

"Yeah." Jaxson shrugged sheepishly. "I haven't decided on what make, what model. I'll have to have my hands on the wheel before I can pick. It has to be affordable—my kind of affordable. I don't know, something used. Maybe a Malibu, heated seats would be a bonus."

Mr. Walters laughed. "We're getting you a Camaro."

"Uh… okay?"

Jaxson couldn't wipe the stupid grin off his face, roaring around town in his brand spanking new, latest model, all the bells and whistles included, Chevrolet Camaro. Jaxson had the pride of paying for most of it, while his boss gave him a considerable bonus to cover the rest. This was the second time in his life he experienced such a bold gesture of generosity, and he didn't know how to respond, besides overwhelming gratitude. When Jaxson stepped out into the carport next to his house, his body was shaking.

He ran up to the mansion and knocked on their front door. Mr. Walters, returning home sooner, answered.

"Can I talk to Brook?"

"Certainly."

Jaxson slipped off his shoes and ran up the stairs. "Brook. Brook," he called out repeatedly. "Can I use your phone? I have to call Melanie." He couldn't wait in the dark anymore. Bryson was on their tail, constantly suspicious his sister would sneak off, and Jaxson knew she wanted to. "I have to show her my new car."

"New car?" Brooklyn opened the door. Her bedroom was in shambles. Clothes were tossed everywhere, hanging off the closet, the four-post bed frame, and another shirt flew into the air and fell onto him. She peeked out the window, "Ooh sexy." She swatted his chest. "Look at you, all grown up. Hey um," she patted her neck. "You haven't seen my necklace have you?"

"Which one?"

"The one I always wear." Jaxson raised his brows at her comment, until she corrected herself, "The one I wear usually. It's white gold and it has little teardrop diamonds—tiny ones, but they're real. It has a cute heart pendant that's pink. Oh man! This is terrible. Mom is going to freak out if she finds out I lost it. I promised Collette I would wear it for the wedding this weekend."

Jaxson tilted his head, "Did you say diamond?"

"Yeah. It was white-gold and had real diamonds."

"Is anything else missing?" he asked, staring at the room in disarray. "Did you make this mess?"

"Of course. I'm freaking out. I wore it to my date last night, but I don't know where I put it afterwards."

"Your date?" Jaxson pulled back the upholstered chair at her makeup vanity and sat down. "Since when have you been dating?"

"First date. I thought since Collette had Jesse, and Melanie has you, I'd find myself a hunky bad boy, and you'll never guess who I found." Before Jaxson could guess, she blurted, "Your friend, Leo."

"Leo?" His eyes bugged out. He wouldn't call Leo a friend, not anymore—maybe an enabler. He was the one who handed him his first opioid. "Let me guess. You kissed him, didn't you?"

She nodded, hands clasped together, blushing in reverie.

"Tell me everything, now!" he growled.

"Whoa. No need to get hasty." She giggled. "He took me to Lakeside Grill, only the fanciest restaurant around.

"Did he go to the washroom?"

"Yeah, but he returned."

"After he hugged you, am I right?"

"Kissed me on the cheek, yes."

"Who paid?"

"Him, of course."

"How?"

"Credit card."

Jaxson clenched his fists. "Brooklyn, check your accounts right now."

She opened the mobile banking app on her phone with a perplexed expression on her face.

"Leo isn't my friend, not anymore. Who paid for the meal?"

When the page loaded, her mouth gaped. "I did. He used my credit card." She closed the app, then slipped her phone back into her pocket. "He stole my necklace too, didn't he? I'm never going to get it back." Her eyes watered. Soon mascara-soaked tears trickled down her cheeks, ruining her time-consuming makeup job. "I have to call the cops."

"No," Jaxson blurted. "Let me talk to him. They'll just put a dent on his record. I'll smack some sense into him and I'll find you that necklace. I promise."

Brooklyn's lip quivered. "You would do that for me?"

"Yeah, you're family. Cancel your card, I'll fix this; just don't tell anyone okay?"

Jaxson twirled his ball cap around his head and stamped down the carpeted stairs. Leo was a bad guy alright, and he had a bad side Jaxson didn't want her to get sucked into. He slid into his new car, flicking his shades down, and ripped out of the driveway to Laney's Bar. Jesse would freak out if he found out he was in contact with his old pal Leo again, especially after worrying him with the recent health emergency.

The pink neon light flickered, and the L had been dead for years. The vinyl siding had broken off in sections, and the entire back of the building was spray painted in meaningless amateur insignia.

He took a deep breath and clenched the steering wheel tight. His many vices were all intermingled in the one dark tavern. Closing his eyes, he remembered Melanie's encouraging words, "I'm proud of you." She could have said anything else, yet there she had done it again, being too good for a sore loser like him.

Showing off his sick new ride and ticking off the hotshot lawyer to drive off into the sunset would have to wait.

Jaxson hopped out of the car, adjusted his shirt, then walked in like he had a hundred times before. Heads turned. Jaws dropped. Old friends crowded around the pool table, placing cash bets on the game. The bartender raised his brow.

"Long time, no see, Jax. How's Nessie?" he asked.

"That ended ages ago. Where are you getting your news?"

"I'm not apparently. What will it be?"

Jaxson shook his hand, "Where's Leo?"

Upon hearing his name, blond hair, green-eyed Leo passed on his cue stick to his latest groupie. He walked right up to his face and eyed Jaxson head to toe.

"Look who decided to show. You know, I've got a pal in the big city. Milton Gore. He's got his own gang, but he's looking for fresh talent. Pay is huge. Straight out of jail, just like you. I'll put in a word."

"I heard about your hot date," Jaxson said, purposely changing the subject. He wasn't there for idle chit-chat, rather he was a man on a mission.

"Real hot date, yeah. We have plans this weekend too."

"Not anymore," Jaxson growled, "Don't bull with me. Where's the necklace?" He became more agitated by the second. The lingering stench of cigarette smoke blew in from the back doors. Black lights lit the room with neon liquor signs reflecting off the bottles displayed behind the bartender.

"I don't know what you're talking about."

Jaxson gripped him by his shirt and threatened to slam his spine into the tiled countertop. It was a black band t-shirt with the sleeves torn off.

"Where is the necklace?"

"I don't have it."

"Then who does?"

"I sold it." Leo grinned. Jaxson released his ex-friend, and wiped a hand down his face. He had a garbage reputation with the local pawnshop dealer. A part of him wanted to catch up with his other so-called friends in the pub, but that part was repulsed at the guy who used to fit in with this crowd.

"What are you doing, man? Do you want to get screwed over like me? Stop." His friend shrugged which made him groan. "Dude, you pick-pocketed your girlfriend… on the first date. You have a problem." He couldn't stomach another second of the place and stormed off.

Chapter 11

"I realize you're upset with me, but I'll make it up to you," Bryson said over the phone. "I've booked us a reservation at the Lakeside Grill, best seat in the house. Dress up though, okay? They have a dress code there. If you don't, you'll stand out and not in a good way." He ended the call, leaving Melanie to prepare for their special dinner out together.

The feud between them had gone on long enough. She loved her brother, faults and all, but this arguing had to end. Perhaps this would be their first step to peace. With a few kind words, maybe she could finally convince him to give Jaxson a chance. She hadn't seen him in person since the day he landed in the Emergency Room, but she had heard through Brooklyn, that the distance he kept between them was related to his nerves.

Bryson had scared Jaxson spit-less, and as much as he wanted to see Melanie, he couldn't afford being arrested again, especially before his brother's wedding. However the wedding was in a few short days, which meant they would have to reconnect, and she would have another whole evening to appreciate him looking irresistibly delicious in an expensive suit.

She thought about visiting Jaxson between her shifts like before, however betraying her brother worse than she already had, didn't settle well on her conscience. She hoped Jaxson could forgive her, but her family had been by her bedside when she was at her worst.

Through chemo, through school, through thick and thin, Bryson had been there for her.

As brother and sister, they needed this. If Bryson said he would make it up to her, she wouldn't miss it for the world. Their parents were already separated, she didn't want more division within her family.

She touched up her makeup, sticking to neutrals for a down-to-earth look. She flipped through multiple outfits, finalizing on a checkered spaghetti strap dress. The hem was frilly, and it had an adorable bow on the waist. Usually she wore it with a sheer t-shirt underneath, but it had been so ridiculously hot these last few summer nights, she decided to go without, but after her concert fiasco, decided to slip on a pair of athletic shorts underneath. No one would see them, but they gave her the assurance she needed.

She hemmed and hawed over what shoes to wear, deciding to pick a comfortable pair of sneakers for her long walk downtown.

"Under Bryson Duong?" she said to the restaurant hostess.

"Right this way," the woman dressed professionally head to toe in black said, led her to the far end of the restaurant. The closed off section had floor to ceiling windows facing the glimmering lake below to the majestic view. The sun was about to set. Its warm rays reflected off the calm blue water lined by forests and luxury homes. A heron flew over the surface, while a larger fish jumped farther away.

As the hostess walked away, metal legs scraped the floor. Melanie turned sharply. Her eyes widened to Rhett.

"Hey."

"What are you—oh." She gritted her teeth, though her stomach growled, preventing her from darting out that very second. The early shift and long walk had brought a mighty appetite. "Bryson isn't going to show, is he?" She sat down begrudgingly.

Rhett shook his head, grinning proudly. "Nope. Wine?"

"No thanks," she said, thinking about Jaxson's sobriety and how she would gladly encourage him by going along too, but it was too late. Rhett refilled his glass and poured some in hers.

"This isn't a date," she blurted, reaching for the breadstick and dipping it in the marinara sauce. "You're my brother's friend and this is us hanging out at the very most."

"Sure, whatever you want to call it." He teased another grin. "Cute outfit." His tongue laced over the top row of his blindingly white teeth. "What would you like to have?" Lowering his voice, he added, "Money is no object."

"I'm not interested," she mumbled, staring at the menu, though she was tempted to order an excessive amount of food, only to have it as leftovers for the next day—including dessert.

"I am, and I don't think you get it, Melanie. I like you and I want you, and if you want I could tell you how, but I think you're a little too innocent to hear that on an empty stomach."

"I have a boyfriend."

"No, you don't. Bryson told me you'd say that too." Rhett brushed his fingers through his bangs. His hair wasn't as heavily gelled as it was on their previous ambushed blind date. He must have switched it out for mousse, since it appeared softer and far more natural. "It's an easy relationship. I give you whatever you want, and in return I ask for the same—starting tonight."

The way his smirk crept up his cheek turned her stomach sour.

"No, I actually have a boy—"

"And my family has a private jet. I could fly you anywhere, anytime. You can ditch your nursing job and live the highlife with me. You want a car? Done. You want to hit up downtown Metropolis and spend the entire weekend shopping, done and done."

"Rhett, the relationship you want from me, I don't think it's healthy. Money corrupts people, whether they have a lot or a little, and I don't think you want a woman who uses you for it."

"You're right," he said with a locked gaze on her. "You truly are an admirable woman, Melanie Duong."

She shook her head. "I'm sorry." She picked up her purse. As she stood, he stepped in front of her, holding out a black credit card.

"It's too late. I already have your brother's blessing, and you know how he is." Rhett tsked. "You're already mine." He placed the card in her hand. She shook her head, trying to return it, but he refused. "Sit," he commanded with a dark undertone.

She scowled fiercely.

"Sit," he repeated.

Intimidated by him, she followed the command with hesitancy, seating herself on the edge of her chair, one foot angled to the door.

"You walked here, didn't you?" Rhett swirled the wine in his glass. "And it was Bryson who drove you to the concert."

"I don't have a car," she mumbled.

"No, you had two." Rhett placed his glass down and leaned forward. "Daddy Duong cut you off, didn't he?" Melanie's mouth gaped, and the slick grin widened, deepening his right dimple. "You're not working because you want to, it's because you have to. Daddy has your trust fund locked far, far out of your reach. Bryson has no clue that's the real reason you're living with him, does he? Why you chose to live in this small town over the city. You can't afford the life you used to have."

"No."

"I know for Bryson, it is pride. He wants to be better than your daddy, but you? Don't think for one minute you have me fooled with this, 'I don't need money' act."

"You're wrong."

"Does Bryson know your driver's license didn't expire, it was revoked?" He swirled the wine in his glass. The first accident may have involved copious amounts of alcohol, but she was much younger then. She was angry from her father's absence. "You're close, you two, aren't you? As a man determined on seeking the truth, wouldn't he be upset if he found out you lied to him?"

"This is blackmail."

"No, it is freedom." He tsked again. "Wouldn't it be great if you had a lawyer on your side, someone who could help you access those funds again? Someone who could help you with your driving situation, and offer you a car and the lessons to boost your confidence? Someone who understands you, this life you're trying to mask. Big money could solve big problems, Melanie."

He removed his gold watch and placed it on the table, between them.

"This was the first thing you noticed about me. Money does matter to you and your brother chose me for a reason. He can't take care of you forever. He has his own life to live."

"I don't want you or your money."

"The hospital could use a considerable donation. Anyone could be a nurse, not everyone could be a philanthropist. You have a heart of gold, Melanie. Why don't you decide where the funds go?"

"Again, this is blackmail."

"No, I'm offering ideas."

"Here's an idea. Why don't you take this card and put it where it belongs, right up your—" She threw the plastic card on the table. He slid it across the tablecloth back to her. This was straight up manipulation. Her workplace could use donations, but he didn't need her to accomplish benevolence.

"Didn't you spend enough time in a hospital? Why not enjoy life for all its fun and frills?"

"I want to give back."

"Then give back. I imagine the cancer ward could use your help. You already suffered. Let's enjoy life… for all its worth." This was a violation of her privacy. If she wanted to tell him her cancer story, she would have. "Take the card." Rhett had no intention of quitting, did he?

"Fine!" She hissed. "I'll take the card, but I'm cutting it up the moment I get home. This wasn't a date. This was an ambush. Goodbye." Before she would cut it, she could use it to prove to Bryson how truly vile his coworker was. The evidence was in her hands. Was Rhett a clever lawyer? Yes. But like her brother said, he was second-best in the office. Bryson was better.

She swiped the remaining breadsticks then marched out, taking a deep breath in the humid air.

Across the street she heard someone banging against the pawn shop window.

"Even if I did have it, I wouldn't sell it to you, but I already told you I don't have it." The storekeeper yelled through the door he held open by a mere crack.

"But Leo came yesterday or today, right?" She could recognize Jaxson's voice from a mile away.

"No. I don't let Leo or any of your friends in this store, and I haven't for the last year."

"Then where does he go?"

"You would know better than me, you're the lawbreaker."

Jaxson spun around frustrated, pounding the door again. He jumped back apologetically from the loud sound, then stomped forward to a shiny Camaro.

Since when could Jaxson afford a high-end model car? And why was he at a pawn shop. She had always avoided those types of stores, because Bryson said they fuelled the crime industry, so she could never ease her conscience on buying something that may have been robbed from someone else.

Doubt drifted through her mind. Though their last conversation had gone well, they hadn't checked up on each other since. The one before was disastrous. He was on edge. He had a history of not sitting still, and the doctor told him to take it easy.

She didn't want to explain the whole Rhett situation, but after the disturbing encounter, she needed Jaxson more than ever. Between the two lawyers, she felt powerless. If not with their words, their actions could force her to become anything they wanted her to be.

Melanie jaywalked across the empty street towards the pawnshop door. Whatever Jaxson couldn't obtain, she could, but she was intercepted. Rhett's hand gripped her wrist and dragged her to the nearby alley.

"Where are you going? That's the wrong car."

"I'm going home."

"Mm-hmm." He said unconvinced. Was this a game to him? She was serious. She should have dumped her glass of wine on him while she had the chance. He cornered her to the siding. Her shoulder blades brushed the cool metal. "I know where your brother lives and you're headed in the wrong direction." He leveled his face with hers, dipping his nose in her loose locks of dark chocolate hair. "Is that vanilla?" He growled hungrily in her ear, "Come, we'll have the food delivered instead."

She whimpered, raising her hands to his chest to push him away, but she was outmatched in both height and strength. "I'm not interested. I really do have a boyfriend. Please don't." She didn't know how she could tell her brother, but tonight left her no other option. He would have to lose a friend—a really powerful, affluent one.

"Move!" Jaxson snapped.

Rhett's grip tightened around her waist, his little roar hadn't intimidated him in the least.

"She's my date."

Melanie caught Jaxson's confused expression, but he shook it off quickly. She pleaded for him with her eyes, begging for his rescue.

He reached for the back of Rhett's shirt and yanked him off her. Rhett caught his footing, not falling backwards, but shoved him into the other wall. In a split second, he gripped Melanie's wrist. She yelped, being dragged in the opposite direction she intended to go.

The resolve in Jaxson's face cracked. He charged Rhett full on, tackling him to the ground. Raising his fist, he smacked him clean in the jaw. Rhett's hands clenched around his throat.

Jaxson choked, clawing at his hands. Seconds which felt like minutes later, he managed to rip Rhett's arm away, and gasped for air.

"You'll never amount to anything. You'll always be bottom of the barrel, scraping and scrounging, Mr. Thorne. You will never have enough for her. She will never be satisfied with you. Don't even try."

Jaxson's lip quivered. "Have we met?"

Rhett slammed into him, tossing him onto his back, then ran off. Jaxson stood to chase him, except Melanie caught his arm.

"I swear, Mel, if that guy goes near you again, he's going to wish he was never alive. I will make his life a living..." He steadied his breath, then pulled her into a hug, inspected each feature on her face for wounds. "Who was that guy?" He kissed her hair. "Am I ever glad I was here. Whoa, that was too close. Okay, I really need to get a phone now."

Melanie hushed him, placing a finger over his lips.

"I'm much better now," she wiped the specks of blood off his cheek. "I'm going to call the cops."

"No!" Jaxson pulled her phone down.

"But he just attacked me. Look what he did to you." She was shaking.

"This I can handle. This is just... doing the right thing, but they won't see it that way. They have my record. In their eyes, I'm automatically in the wrong. I want justice as much as you, if not more, but all it takes is one little thing and I'm back behind bars."

"I won't let that happen to you, Jaxson."

He kissed her hair again, stroking the back of her head, "I'll take care of this, I promise. I'll deal with that guy, one on one, later. I'll make him wish he were never born. No one lays a hand on my woman."

"Don't become a brute."

"No. This is a conversation we need to have. Man to man. He needs to know."

"Or we could have the legal system deal with it—justly."

"That's the lawyer, right?" He groaned. "He knows the loopholes. Police can make their arrest, but it is guys like him that choose the punishment. And it is always the guys like me who suffer. Promise me you won't call the cops."

Melanie stared into his concerned eyes for a full minute. She thought about her brother and his hatred towards criminals. This was more than fear. It was experience. Jaxson meant every word, and would risk life and limb to protect her.

She linked her pinkie with his, confirming her promise. "What are you doing here anyways?"

"I came to find Brooklyn's necklace. She dated an *old* friend of mine," he raised his brows to emphasize the word, 'old,' then continued. "He pawned it off, and if it isn't here, then it's in the city. If I leave now, I might make it in time before they close. If I call, they might reserve it, but what luck would I have?"

Melanie watched a shopper step out of the pawn shop. Huh, so they only locked Jaxson out.

"Let me come with you."

"It's a long trip. I'm not planning on doing anything else when I arrive. Get there. Get back. Plus Teagan hates me, so you don't want to be around to witness it."

"All the more reason you'll need me."

Jaxson pursed his lips. "Fine."

"Fine?"

"Yeah, fine. You're so beautiful you could sell rain to the clouds, sand to the nomads, ice to the polar bears. It's not a bad idea." What was with his unconvinced tone?

"But?"

"What about your brother?" he asked, gesturing between the two of them.

"My brother set me up with him." She jerked her thumb in the direction Rhett ran off to. "You let me deal with him. I'm an adult woman. I don't have to work until the day after your brother's wedding, and we haven't been on a single date. That sir, is a crime."

Jaxson shrugged. "I am a criminal."

Her teeth grazed her lower lip. "You could have had me fooled. Now explain that." She pointed to the car. He chuckled, wrapping his arm behind her waist, leading her in for a closer look.

Jaxson rattled the pawn shop's doors, seething. "Closed? Closed? They're a pawn shop. They're supposed to be open late. I swear they used to be open all night."

"Calm down." Melanie brushed her hand against his chest. His heart beat wildly against her palm. "We'll leave them a message. We could ask to reserve the necklace."

"No. Teagan doesn't roll that way."

"You've been here before."

Jaxson scratched the back of his neck, "Yeah. Whenever we'd arouse suspicion, we'd make the drive. Teagan buys off you cheaper, but he never asks questions, and when you're desperate…"

"We don't have to talk about it." Melanie patted his chest again. "We'll just have to come first thing tomorrow. When do they open?" She squinted at the sign. "Ten o'clock. Okay."

"You don't have to join me. Thanks for accompanying me, but—"

"I was thinking we could book a hotel."

"A hotel?" Jaxson licked his lips, then peeked over her shoulder. The frustration he had a moment ago, picked up its wings and flew away. "Right." He cleared his throat, "Separate beds of course."

"Of course," she purred, wrapping her arms around his shoulders, she pecked the edge of his lips. As she was going to expand on the kiss, her stomach gurgled. "Perhaps we should pick up dinner on the way?"

Returning to the vehicle, she focused on her phone, searching hotels as Jaxson strolled through the city. At the late hour, each place they drove by disappointed them with a closed sign, not that he was hungry anymore. Her little comment had his appetite elsewhere.

His gaze flicked to the fuel gauge on his dash, "You know what place is open? It's no steak and lobsters, but they make a mean taquito." He pulled up to the gas station, and fuelled up the car. Afterwards, they went inside together.

"I know it's not super romantic, but I used to crave this stuff like all the time." He opened the cooler and picked out a Jones soda for him and her. She walked through the aisles for toiletries, then met him at the food warmer. The ordered a pizza slice, taquitos, chicken strips, and spicy wedges.

Jaxson opened his wallet at the register, but Melanie beat him to it, pulling out a black credit card.

"It's on me," she held a teasing grin he found suspicious. He took a deep breath, and let her pay, carrying the food for them to the car.

"No eating in the car," he said, catching her hand fishing through the bag on her lap.

"What about licking?" She tucked the driblet of sauce off her fingers.

"You're trouble."

"And you're a trouble-maker."

Jaxson choked on his spit, pulling onto the highway. Either she was fully aware of the tricks she played on him, or she was miraculously blessed with an abundance of child-like innocence. In the past, love had entertained him, and having someone he could tolerate for longer periods of time was more than pleasant, but he had spent so much time absorbed in the past or the woes of the present, he hadn't taken a moment to consider the future.

Jesse was going to be married and have his future soon, but happily ever after was more than a ring, it was a lifetime shared with the person he would give that ring to. Often, the love story would expand. Newlyweds often became parents, and perhaps if they were ever in the position to raise a child or two bratty boys, he would want to have a woman like Melanie by his side.

Encouraging him at his lowest, calming him in the heat of the moment, warning him before the trouble hits, and straight up being adorable, he loved her.

"I love you," she said, "I just felt like you needed to hear that."

Her words only confirmed his feelings about her, still, she had been acting strange.

"Please tell me the motel is near."

"Hotel." She pointed to the brick building with the black awning.

"That's out of my price range."

"My treat," she said, waving her black credit card.

"Are you sure? I know nurses are paid well, but not that well. Seriously, I can sleep on the couch, a cot. I don't need a pillow. I'll pass out just about anywhere."

"It's too late. You deserve to have the royal treatment after what you've been through."

"I don't."

"Yes, you do." She jabbed her finger in his arm. "Don't fight me."

"I wouldn't dream of it." He smirked, then pulled in to the lobby entrance. Melanie ran inside to check in as he found a parking spot. When he met her inside, carrying the food with him, she led him to the elevator, passing the black leather couches and crystal chandeliers.

Outside their room, he paused.

"What is it?" Melanie asked.

"I don't belong here."

"Why?"

Jaxson picked at the back of his neck. "I spent months in a cell the same width as this hallway." He thought about Mr. Walters' generosity, and how the love of his life was about to open the door to an opulent space he could and never would be able to afford.

Melanie pressed a smile, and tugged on his wrist, pulling him inside their room.

He double blinked in disbelief. Immediately he was greeted with a trail of red rose petals leading to a king size bed with white bedding. Across from it was a Jacuzzi tub. On the table was a bucket full of ice, with a bottle of champagne. A box of chocolate covered strawberries laid next to it.

"What is this?"

Melanie's shoulders hunched, avoiding his piercing gaze. He stood closer, kicking his shoes off.

"Mel?" He crooked an eyebrow.

"The honeymoon package." She smiled guiltily, like it would squeeze her out of trouble. Fortunately, he found her irresistibly adorable.

"Mm-hmm." He dunked the sodas in the ice bucket next to the champagne bottle. He dropped the warm food next to it, hastily, closing the gap between them. His hands slipped in her hair. He pulled the silly hibiscus flower clip out of her bangs, and captured her mouth.

The hours driving next to her, listening to her overly innocent comments, after the weeks of silence, snapped him. The gentleman vanished and his weight collapsed over her.

She smiled in his aggression. Purring as he caressed a rose petal under her nose, then brushing the velvety texture along her rosy cheeks.

"You're a lover," she whispered. Her eyes closed, lost in the ecstasy of his touch.

"You're a healer," he murmured in response, removing the cards from her pockets. He flicked the key to the carpet, then winced at the credit card. "Who is Rhett C. Brinkley?"

Chapter 12

Melanie sat up, flushed in the face, staring at the dark expression on Jaxson's face. He looked as if he was about to snap the card in a split second.

"This is wrong."

"Yes, but I can explain."

"You're using money that isn't yours. That is what society calls stealing." He expelled a heavy breath, disappointed in her. "I knew I corrupted you, but I didn't think it would be like this." He slapped the card on the table, then brought the food to her.

Whatever mood they had was hit by a car.

"Ladies first." Opening the box, he held out the chicken strips to her.

She took a bite and winced.

"Oh, it's not that bad. Sure it's not lobster, but..." he grabbed a piece for himself, and forced it down. "I don't remember them being this greasy. I used to crave these all the time."

"When you were high?"

Jaxson closed the box. "That may or may not have been a factor." He mowed down the taquitos anyway. "Credit card. Explain."

"Rhett was the guy you punched. He gave it to me."

"Still wrong." He glanced around the room. "But no more." His blue-grey eyes glinted with mischief. "Wait. Why did he give you a credit card?"

Melanie rolled her eyes, "So he could exploit me, I guess. I don't know. I told him I was going to cut it up when I got home, but since I'm not home…" she let the comment trail off.

"You are trouble. I was horribly mistaken to think you were a good girl. You're far from it, fooling all of us."

"If only I could reason with Bryson. He's the one that keeps setting me up on dates with Rhett." Thinking about both Bryson and Rhett made her furious. "He thinks he can act like Dad or something, but I'm an adult. It's so infuriating that he has all this power on me. He wasn't always like this, you know. Before he became a lawyer, he was the fun one. I was the troublemaker."

"That fact hasn't changed. You're still a troublemaker. Fry?"

She shook her head. Jaxson took the rest of the food and tossed it in the trash.

"Why did you think it would be okay to use the card?"

"I don't know. I was angry."

"What happens when he demands payment?"

"Then you can beat him up for me," she giggled. His eyes widened with surprise. Seconds later, he reached around her and tickled her stomach. It gurgled again. "Let's order room service."

"I'm paying," Jaxson demanded, reaching farther to the nightstand. He picked up the menu and his jaw dropped.

She lowered the menu, meeting his eyes. "It gets billed to the room."

"Oh," he said softly. "Just this one time. I'll buy us breakfast. I don't like not paying."

"You want to provide."

"Yes," he admitted. There was a long pause between them. Melanie decided to turn on the TV, flicking through the channels to put on a movie. "I'm sorry I haven't bought you any gifts yet."

"I'd rather spend time with you, than have a trinket wishing you were."

"I may never be able to provide. If the Walters ever fired me, I'd be renting in a trailer with a bunch of guys probably—not the good kind. I want a good job, I really do, but I've got that stupid stain on my record. No one's going to trust me."

"I trust you," Melanie said, snuggling into his torso. "You saved my life today." She felt foolish for giving Rhett the benefit of the doubt, that she could just take the card and leave. He blindsided her with the information and chasing her into the alley. Was Jaxson really okay? His face was blue. There was blood.

After a commercial break, Jaxson sighed, stroking her loose chestnut waves.

"I wouldn't," he mumbled. "I wouldn't trust me. I'm going to mess this up somehow. I know it. That's just how I am. I try, but I always fail. I work hard, I get heatstroke. I'm impulsive." He held the glass pop bottle against his cheek. "Last time I felt this good, felt like I was in love, I stole an engagement ring. It was dumb, but I was never going to afford one. I wasn't in the right state of mind, but then again, who do you know that has acted completely logical when in love? Her name was Genesis, you may have seen her at the engagement party. The old me thought she was a blast. She had attitude, and for a guy who didn't care about the law, I liked her spite. I don't know what I was thinking. We walked into the store together, and I asked her, if money was no object, which one she wanted."

"She picked the most expensive one?"

"Yeah. I should've seen the signs. Wasn't that she was a gold digger, but she liked gifts. She liked it when I'd spend on her, but we were young and stupid."

"We're still young."

"And I'm still stupid."

Melanie smacked his chest. "Stop it. No, you're not." Instead of flinching in pain, he smiled. "You see the world through a different lens than me. I don't care what others say or what lies you tell yourself. This person is good, he is smart, and he is beautiful." Her eyelashes fluttered.

He captured her hand over his chest and dragged it along his torso. Closing the gap between them, he kissed her painfully slow. Desire built in her, like a cable stretching on the verge of snapping.

"You were telling a story."

His lips quirked up. Right, this is what he meant about being impulsive. With a kiss like that, she could welcome more of his distractions.

"She found out I stole it. How could she not, the whole bloody town had. Didn't help I was under the influence at the time, too buzzed to consider the details like, I don't know—the security system. I'm not proud of what I did, but even for a crook, it was utterly embarrassing. Jesse couldn't afford a lawyer. It did more harm than good. Your brother destroyed us—me in the courtroom, sent me off to jail on an impossibly high bail. I felt like garbage, to add to the mix, Genesis decided she was better off without me. There was no ultimatum; she already fell out of love, apparently."

Melanie reached for his hand. He wiped a tear with the other.

"Sorry, it just feels good getting this out."

"Honesty is good." Melanie encouraged him to continue, offering him the tissue box.

"But I'm glad she did." Jaxson watery gaze lowered to hers. "I used to believe I could never love again, never trust a woman, that they were all cold and ruthless, but then I met you. Beautiful, caring, the voice of an angel, and the servitude of one too. If she hadn't broken my heart, I would have never had this. I used to be worried I would want to fall back, but I'm not the guy I used to be. I saw one of my buddies earlier. Before my sentence, he was my best friend, but today when I looked at him, I was repulsed. I have been wronged my whole life, and I've wronged others for it, but if I could do just a little good, I will."

"Which is why you're returning Brooklyn's necklace."

He nodded. This was not a convenient task and she respected him more for it.

"I went years without a father, and today, when Brooklyn's dad drove me to the dealership, I caught a glimpse of what I'd missed out on. He's a really cool guy. I know gardening doesn't pay well, not like a lawyer or nurse or a business manager, but I really want to keep working for him if he gives me the chance." Jaxson glanced around the room. "Which means we might not ever get this again."

"Are you afraid of bad luck or intimidated by good fortune?" Melanie pulled him into a hug. "This is my treat for you. Enjoy it."

Please enjoy it. Guilt pricked at her for pretending. Again, she had told him half-truths, only part of the story of who she was. Hiding her last name was more than the connection to her brother, it was her father. At first, like with anyone else it was a safeguard for her friendships to be genuine and so she wouldn't be used for her money.

Bryson had distanced himself from their family fortune too. He had his reasons, and she assumed they were similar to hers.

She had to tell him. Jaxson had opened his heart to her, poured out the pains he had been grieving for years, yet she held back. Melanie understood him, but she hadn't explained why, but if she did, would he still love her? She almost lost him. She couldn't let go, not after what he did for her.

Room service knocked on their door.

"I should be treating you," he said with a playful grin.

"Every moment with you is a treat." Melanie stuck out her tongue, then jumped off the bed, excited to eat her midnight meal.

When she carted the meal to the bedside, Jaxson crossed his arms. "I know that look, Mel. I can't read your mind, but I know there's something bothering you." Her hand hovered over the metal dish cover, but Jaxson intercepted, slapping his palm over it, holding it down. "Mel?"

"I'm rich…" she gulped, searching for a reaction, but his face hadn't changed. "I mean, my dad is rich."

Jaxson shrugged.

"No like, really *really* rich."

He released his hand and leaned back into the pillows, "I kind of figured. You hinted that when we first met."

"No, like richer than—"

Jaxson planted a smooch on her lips, muting her. His hands found their way in her hair again, a sensation she would never tire of. Tingles shot through her body. "I know," he breathed. "And I don't care. You're worth more."

"How do you know?" she asked baffled, brushing the messy strands of hair out of her face.

"Your brother drives the most expensive car in town. Your clothes aren't cheap. Those shoes were designer label—not a department store knock off either. I stole. I was a thief, Mel. I know the value and the resale value on these items, probably better than you do. You can fool them, but you won't fool me." The back of his fingers stroked the side of her cheek. "Gifts from your dad, right?"

She nodded, welling up with tears.

"Hey," he hushed her tenderly, rubbing his calloused finger under her eye. "You have me." He reached over, removed the metal lid, and revealed her entrée. "Eat. You'll feel better."

She sniffed. Picking up the fork, she stabbed into the flame broiled vegetables. "I had a car too. Two actually. The first one I got as a graduation present. A year later, I was drinking—a rare occurrence by the way—it was to relax, but I only became angrier. It was the second birthday he missed. The first I excused, starting at the company overseas and all, but this one hit hard. My parents were officially separating and my world was falling apart. I worked so hard at school, to enter nursing, and I even beat cancer, but I asked myself, what was it worth? Mom and Dad didn't love each other. Bryson was doing his law school stuff—we weren't a family anymore. I felt so alone."

Melanie slumped into him, resting her head on his shoulder.

"The second car, well… I don't know what got to me. Maybe I was drunk on anger. It seemed like the only way to get my dad's attention was to scare him. Lost my license for it. Obviously it was wrong, and I deserved to have him take away my credit cards, but I never wanted them anyway. I should have never done those stupid things. They weren't going to bring my family together to the way we were before the money corrupted us."

Jaxson kissed her crown, "I used to wonder how I'm still alive, but now I'm asking the same for you. Mel, you are trouble and I have no problem driving you around, until you're ready."

"You would let me drive your new car?"

"No." He smirked. "But I won't let your mistakes hold you back."

"I'll bet it takes a lot of loving to turn a seed into a strawberry patch," Melanie teased, placing the strawberries between them. Her overall mood had improved after their meal, which boosted his. Jaxson had other ideas of dessert, but he plucked one out of the clear carton and fed it to her.

"Have you ever thought about kids?" he asked. *Where did that come from?* Jaxson used to shy away from the idea. With his father out of the picture and his last memories on how he treated his mother, he figured he was the last person on the planet who would step into that level of responsibility willingly.

Responsible was not a word in his vocabulary. He and Jesse were terrorizing demons. In his mind, he wasn't worthy enough to become a parent.

Melanie shoveled the last two strawberries in her mouth. "I mean, sure. Eventually yeah, why not? That's the purpose of dating, right? Find a good partner to start a family with. After marriage of course…" she coughed, but stopped herself from choking. "You seem like a good partner."

Jaxson covered his mouth with his arm, biting it not to burst out in laughter.

"You picture me as a dad?"

"One day, yeah." She cleared the plates then washed her hands. "Hey, if you can keep a plant alive, you could figure it out. For what you can't, you'll have me."

"You want this?" He gestured to himself baffled. Kissing her passionately was one thing, opening up to each other's souls was another, but accepting the chaos imbedded in his DNA was a whole other story.

She chewed her lip and pounced on him. Weakened by her beauty, he refused to be bothered by her misinterpretation.

"Keep this up and we'll never sleep," he warned. Her lips grazed his prominent jaw line. It was one night in the hotel room—one night. He clawed into her dress, at war with himself. One night was all it took to get locked up.

One night found him the love of his life.

One night—or one hot sunny day without water landed him in the ER.

In the heat of the moment, he excused himself and stepped off the bed. "I don't think we should sleep together." With the thoughts racing though his mind, this was the remnant drip of his resolve.

"It's a big bed."

"I sleep naked," he blurted, only half true. Only on warm nights, which this was.

Melanie swallowed, licking her lips. While every other time in their relationship he couldn't read her mind, he could read her body like an open book.

"I move a lot in my sleep." That he couldn't confirm, but if they shared a bed, he would guarantee a lot of movement, sleep—not so much.

"Do you want me to sleep on the couch?" she asked.

He scowled at her, "Absolutely never."

"Good." She grinned. "It's a really comfy bed."

"I won't sleep on the couch or floor either. I won't sleep at all if we're in the same room together." As a recovering addict, he knew his limit. This was the line. "I'm going to shower, then I'll meet you in the morning for breakfast."

"But the Jacuzzi tub… You work so hard. You should at least enjoy a soak."

His eyes trailed to the tub across the room.

"A tub that size, you'd have to join me."

Her lips parted in an 'O' shape, fully understanding the gravity of the situation. "Oh. You're not joking." Her cheeks flushed crimson red.

"Not once." He bopped her nose, "And don't think for one second you fooled me. You are trouble."

Melanie crossed her arms and sunk deeper into the cushions. "I can behave." Except this was the same woman who watched him toil in the garden all summer. Again, he knew his limits, but did she know hers? "I can't behave," she admitted a minute later. "I'm sorry. But I really did pick this room to treat you and I don't know. I thought it wouldn't be that big of a deal, but I was also scared. After what happened tonight, I don't want to sleep alone, yet I want what I'm told I can't have. What if we never—I know better, but I wish…" she exhaled again, visibly wrestling with the temptation.

"We talked about this. You need to tell me no."

"What if I don't want to?"

Jaxson gave her a gentle peck on the lips. "Goodnight, Mel."

Melanie met Jaxson by the door at nine o'clock. He had a brown paper bag with breakfast sandwiches and two orange juices in his hands. There were dark bags under his eyes and he had a dopey grin on his face.

"Good morning, beautiful. Did you sleep well?"

"Like a dream. Did you? Where did you sleep?" she said, setting up the food at the table. Her hair was damp. After a few minutes of using the ear-piercingly loud hairdryer after her shower, she opted for a messy bun. After Jaxson's comment about the Jacuzzi tub, she couldn't will herself to try it, not when he tempted her with that scandalous idea. However, 'beautiful' was pushing it. She wore the same outfit as the day before, only she had no makeup to complete the look, but the integrity in his voice complimented her immensely, proving she could always be herself around him.

"The car," Jaxson said. "The stars were magnifique." He pinched his lips for a chef's kiss.

Strangely, she admired him more for his willpower to say no when he wanted otherwise, proving the significance of his intentions. When the time would come, he would mean it, and it would be worth the wait—even if it pained her. Words like, "I love you," held their weight, like his kisses confirmed they were for more than gratification, they were a genuine outpour of his heart.

After they finished their breakfast, they left the hotel hand in hand and drove to the pawn shop on the other side of the city. Melanie stepped out of the car. The building casted shade over the street and she felt the morning chill nip at her legs.

Jaxson opened the pawn shop door. It was the first time she'd stepped foot in one. There were lower end items like antique furniture, china dishware, and iconic gadgets from previous generations. Walking through the store was magical, like going backwards in time.

She wandered the aisles, aimlessly giving each item a story in her mind. In a locked cabinet were signed records and famous video game cartridges. The consoles and handheld devices brought her to her childhood.

"How much did you give Leo? I'll match it," Jaxson said, tapping the glass case by the register. Teagan raised his eyebrows, dissecting him. The man was a foot shorter than him and at least an additional eighty pounds. He wore an outdated dragon silk shirt and a knockoff Rolex on his wrist.

"You're buying?"

"No. I'm returning. Leo stole that necklace, now I'll pay you back and—"

"Hold up, this is a business here. I can't go off selling things for the same price I bought them."

"Are you kidding me?" Jaxson snarled. "It wasn't his to pawn."

"Takes one to know one," Teagan chided. "Nine hundred, plus tax."

"Nine hundred?" Jaxson exclaimed. He cussed under his breath. When his eyes caught on to Melanie's his cheeks reddened. "Aw, c'mon, man. Cut me a deal. Does it look like I would have that kind of money? I could report you to the cops, and have this place closed for good."

"You? Call the cops? Nine-fifty."

Jaxson spun around, gripping his hair. He stomped down the aisle, probably fighting whatever negative thoughts he had about him or the necklace. Melanie chose to step in, slipping out the black credit card.

"Cash only, ma'am."

She looked up to the sign taped to the register with the same message. The glass case was full of unique and beautiful jewels. A pink sapphire surrounded by smaller diamonds sparkled in the store's fluorescent lighting. She bit her lip, tempted to buy the ring, but then she would have to inconvenience Jaxson to a separate trip to the bank. The price was higher than she would spend on jewelry, but like Jaxson mentioned the previous night, she couldn't afford to get her hopes up, not on her own income.

"My best friend will be devastated without it. That necklace means so much to her." She turned to Jaxson. "You were there when she reported it stolen to the police, right?"

Jaxson shrugged, playing along. "When I found out he pawned it here, I made a mad dash. If the cops were tipped as well, it won't be long before they catch up."

"Well…" Teagan drummed his fingers against the counter. "For eight hundred, I'd still be making a profit, and we could pretend none of this happened."

"Seven fifty," Melanie said, batting her eyelashes.

Teagan scowled. "You're lucky she's pretty," he groveled, removing the necklace from the case. Jaxson opened his wallet to pay, but closed it.

"One second. I've got to make a quick trip to an ATM."

"First come, first serve," Teagan warned.

Outside the store, Jaxson stroked his day-old shave, then gave her a wicked glint. Without a moment's notice, he pulled her into his arms, and kissed her with no restraint. She figured at most, he was going to give her a high five or a brief, "Thank you," but this was something else. It sparked bolts of electricity through her body. Was it because they were in public? Was it his impulsive or careless nature?

His hands roamed her body, though she was too distracted by the tricks of his tongue. She would definitely continue assisting him, if this was the thanks he offered.

He stepped back and licked his lips. "Have you bought a gift for the wedding yet?" His eyes flicked to the gift shops across the street. "Now is your chance."

"Oh! That's a good idea." Were they going to pretend they didn't just make out for the last five minutes? Okay, cool, whatever. She nervously wiped her sweaty palms down the skirt of her dress. "Should I pick up anything on your behalf? Joined gift?"

He shook his head, "I'll just pop over to the bank. See you soon?"

She skipped across the street, entering the environmentally-conscious home décor shop. Most of the products were items she would see scrolling online, but she couldn't remember Collette's taste when it came to interior design, so she figured it would be best to text Brooklyn, maybe send some pictures. She reached into her purse, but when she fished for her phone, it wasn't there.

Chapter 13

Around the corner of the pawn shop, out of Melanie's line of sight, he punched in the password to her phone and dialed his brother's number. He held the device to his ear, waiting for him to pick up.

"Hello?" Jesse asked in a 'who's this?' fashion.

"Yo. I need two hundred bucks."

"You what—no."

"I promise I'll pay you back."

"No Jax. No way. Where are you?"

"It doesn't matter, just email me two hundred, three, just to be safe."

"Safe?" Jesse snapped. "You disappeared and you're asking me for money. No. Don't do this to me. You were doing so good. Clean for a whole year—don't ruin this. You can walk away now. Not before the wedding, man. You're all I have left."

"Calm down."

"How can I calm down? What if you OD? What do I do then?"

"OD on what? I need it to buy a ring."

"To buy a what? Excuse my French, but what's that code for these days? Pardon me for not being with the times."

"A ring—like an engagement ring."

"For who?"

Jaxson rolled his eyes. Was his brother playing dumb? "For Melanie." Who else?

"Melanie? As in Melanie Duong? Do you have a death wish? You're still together? Need I remind you the mess you got in with your last choice?"

"This is different. I don't know when, but I know she is the one this time. For real. Stuck up brother or not, I'll find a way around it. Please. I'm short on funds. I just bought a car and I didn't plan on it, but it's there. I saw it. She couldn't keep her eyes off it... I have to get her that ring."

"Didn't you learn your lesson at all?"

"Hey! You said I shouldn't pass up on the one."

"I meant to get out of your slump, not marriage. You can't just pop the question. You have to work up to it. Not everyone is like you."

"But she loves me and I love her—I really love her."

Jesse groaned. Jaxson imagined him wiping a palm down his face, pacing around during the moment of silence he waited eagerly for a response. "Can't it be one or two-hundred dollars cheaper?"

"Would you do that to Collette?"

Jesse growled. "Fine, if two hundred dollars saves me from bailing your sorry derriere out of jail, so be it. Oh and you can't steal the spotlight on the big day. And I want it in cash the day I return from our honeymoon!"

"Done and done." Jaxson hung up and deleted the conversation from her call history. His heart fluttered in his chest. Driving to the nearest bank, he withdrew the given amount, then rushed back to the pawn shop. Melanie didn't have to bargain Teagan down, but since she had, he could add the ring to his purchase.

"Receipt?"

"For the necklace."

"Not the ring?"

He shook his head. "Can't have evidence. I want it to be a surprise." He grinned, staring in the direction of the store Melanie was in.

Teagan chuckled. "Here." He shoved the ring in a velvet box. "Got a million of these suckers collecting dust in the back. No hard feelings, eh?"

"Yeah, yeah." Jaxson waved him off. The man only cared about money. He pocketed the items in his shorts, thankful they were baggy enough to conceal the shapes.

Melanie greeted him across the street with an arm full of bags.

"With your own money?"

She nodded. "Yep. Although before we head home, I think we need to go back to the hotel. I must have left my phone in the room."

About to open the passenger door for her, he slipped his left hand around her back, for another vigorous kiss like the one before. Distracting her with his aggressive affections, he dropped the phone back into her purse, taking longer than he planned because of the angle of the zipper.

He pulled back, stroking her arm, "Are you sure? Maybe you should check again, just in case."

Melanie unzipped her purse, shoved her hand in the bag, and gasped.

"Wow, how did I not see it? Thank goodness. I was really worried there."

Jaxson shrugged. The guilt tugged at him momentarily, but when she would see the ring, as in the same pink sapphire one she picked out, she would without a doubt forgive him. Now all he had to do was to get on Bryson's good side.

"Want to hold onto this for me?" he handed her the receipt, figuring it would be better kept in her purse. He should have given her the necklace, but he didn't want to attract attention to that particular pocket and prematurely reveal the surprise.

A police cruiser pulled into one of the limited parking spaces less than a block away. His body tensed up, it often did whenever he caught sight of one driving by. His instinct was to run and hide, except Melanie must have read his apprehension and caught his wrist.

"Don't. It will only make you look guilty."

He exhaled slowly, yet his heart raced a million beats a minute. The late morning sun shone over him. Angling his cap didn't help, he was sweating bullets. He would cover his eyes too, but he left the shades in the car.

The officers walked into the pawn shop.

"Did you call them?" he asked.

She shook her head. "Did you?"

The assisting officer peered out the window, his eyes widening at Jaxson. He reached for his radio, mumbling something.

"He's talking on his radio…" Jaxson was jumpy. He tugged at his arm, but Melanie clawed her fingers deeper into his skin, prompting him to remain calm. "They're looking at me."

"And you did nothing wrong."

"It doesn't matter to them."

"Yes, it does. The system is designed to enforce justice and protect the people as long as you abide with the rules. Jax, stand down."

Both officers hustled out of the pawn shop, pacing quickly towards them.

Jaxson freed himself from her grip, to hold onto her hand, fingers locked. His mind was a mess. The stress overwhelmed him, yet she stood there beside him with a calming smile, and it would be all he needed to get through this.

"Jaxson Thorne?"

He pressed his lips together, unwilling to answer them.

"Subject found. The girl is with him, over." The woman with mousy brown hair said into her radio as the taller bulkier male officer separated him from Melanie. She announced who they were then directed the conversation solely on Jaxson, "You're going to have to come to the station."

The man patted him down, searching his pockets, first pulling out his wallet, keys, and the necklace. He placed them on the roof of the Camaro.

"I bought that," Jaxson defended, "She has the receipt."

Melanie held it out. The female officer read through it.

"And this?" The other officer asked, showing off the pink sapphire ring, whistling heartlessly. "Looks expensive. Do you have the receipt for this one?"

Melanie's jaw dropped.

"No." Jaxson's expression dropped. There goes the surprise. He had planned to hold on to it for a while, perhaps until Thanksgiving or Christmas. In his mind the decision was made, but waiting seemed like the responsible thing to do. "I didn't steal it. I swear. I paid for it in full, in cash. I—it's yours, Melanie, if you'll have me. I love you."

His arms were tugged behind his back, as handcuffs were clipped over his wrists.

"Jaxson Thorne you are under arrest for aggravated assault, battery, abduction, and theft." The officer began reciting his rights.

"Lawyer," Jax said. Going through this before, he knew this time, it was best to cooperate, and to demand the lawyer up front. With a steady gaze on her, Melanie nodded back. She would know exactly who to call.

Chapter 14

After Melanie gave her honest testimony, she had to bus home, shivering in her spaghetti strap dress and her shopping bags beside her. Bryson refused to show, leaving her to call Brooklyn, to call Jesse to find a lawyer to defend him less than two days before his wedding.

Boy, did she have an earful to unleash on her 'prosecuting' lawyer brother.

Her innocent boyfriend was locked up in the station until further notice, destined to miss Jesse and Collette's wedding. How was it, she could have the most romantic night of her life, then have all hope of happily ever after thrown in the trash. Life wasn't fair, but did it have to be cruel as well?

A chill nipped her legs during the ride, as rain gushed outside, splattering massive ugly droplets of water against the window panes. The bus stop was two blocks away from her apartment, so she made a mad dash through the torrential rain pour. Her runners slapped the puddles, soaking in the murky water.

She didn't care.

She was furious. Is this what he got after cleaning his life up? No.

And the ring? He actually bought it. She hadn't said a word, yet he knew. He had to have paid for it. She couldn't figure out how, but she believed in the innermost parts of her heart, he would not repeat the same mistake twice, not this man he had become.

Melanie rushed inside, changed into a pair of sweats. She gripped the drawstrings of her sweatshirt, fell onto her bed, and curled into a ball.

"Yes," she cried to herself. Tears streaked her face. "Yes, a thousand times, yes." She imagined the ring in her fist. Fear fueled her agony. With his history and previous jail time, who would believe him? She didn't understand the legal system like her brother except she figured whatever sentence Jaxson would be given would increase in severity because of his previous offense.

As furious as she was at her brother, she needed a bloody incredible lawyer. Even if he wouldn't comply, she would have to pray for a miracle.

Wiping away the tears, she took a deep breath, and put on her game face.

"Hey," Rhett greeted, flashing her with his million-dollar smile that surely would have any other woman complying with his repulsive demands. His jaw was swollen on the right side, mainly green, with flecks of purple, where Jaxson's knuckles met his face.

Good.

Melanie managed to clean herself up before storming into their legal office. A woman didn't go into war in her sweats, and she most definitely wore the proper bra.

"Get lost," she pushed past him, and swung Bryson's door open, inconsiderate to his privacy.

"Melanie!" Bryson jumped away from his desk and rushed to give her a hug. "Are you okay?"

"Am I okay? Are you—are you... you're unbelievable, you know that?" She smacked his face with the back of her hand. "The love of my life is sleeping in a station cell tonight for crimes he did not commit. You have the power and word-lingo magic to free him and you won't. You know what that makes you?"

"He is not the love of your life."

"He is. And he would be my fiancé if those officers didn't confiscate the ring—which he didn't steal. I'd bet everything I have on it. Call the owner of the pawn shop. That ring was locked and secure. It was daytime and the owner was right there, meaning the only way to for Jax to have it, is if he bought it."

She ignored the idea there was a chance the ring could have been reported missing around the time it was pawned, considering how shady Teagan ran his business.

"Need my help?" Rhett offered, but Melanie was quick to slam the door in his face.

Bryson's eyebrows shot up. "Time of the month?"

Melanie took a deep breath. Screaming at her brother was no way to earn his allegiance.

He pulled out a chair for her. "We won't talk until you sit down." She hesitantly took the seat and waited for him to return to his. When she opened her mouth, he held his finger up, silencing her. Closing his current case file, he flipped to a fresh page on his legal pad and clicked his pen. "I'm a busy person and I have an appointment in less than an hour. State your case." A slow grin crept up the side of his face. "Before you embarrass yourself any worse, we have evidence."

Her eyebrows pinched together, "How?"

"Because I'm the best. That's how. I don't enter a courtroom empty handed." Bryson crossed his arms impatiently, "Beg all you want, I can't defend Jaxson. We're representing the person he wronged. If I was available, I still wouldn't. Gardeners can't afford me, and I stand by my moral convictions. I am a prosecutor. I prosecute criminals. He is a criminal."

"Was. He is innocent."

"No. You're innocent. You think just because he is charming to you, he couldn't hurt a fly, but like I said, I have proof."

"What proof?"

Bryson angled his computer monitor towards her, opened a video file and clicked the play icon. The black and white grainy CCTV footage only lasted a few seconds. In the clip, Jaxson punched Rhett, then Rhett ran off with a terrified expression. It painted a horrible picture on Jaxson's behalf.

"I was there," Melanie blurted, before assessing what this meant. If she could have Bryson choose Jaxson over Rhett, Jaxson's release could be expedited. "That's not what happened."

"There's more," he added, not giving her a chance to represent her side of the story.

Bryson showed a clip of Jaxson walking in and out of the hotel, sometimes with Melanie and the times without. "Did you see the timestamp?" He clasped his hands together, "Again, how could a gardener afford a hotel like that, especially after purchasing a car—not just any car—a freaking off-the-lot, Camaro, unless..." he smirked. "It seems strange a guy like him could hold a job, gain the Walters' trust, then disappear, conveniently after Brooklyn's necklace had. Whatever story he told you, is just a story. The Walters helped pay for the car. He is charming alright, but let the evidence speak for itself. You don't have to defend him. He can't hurt you if he is behind bars."

"He's not the person I'm afraid of," Melanie shouted. She pointed to the door. "It's him! The only reason Jaxson punched Rhett was because your so-called friend couldn't take 'no' for an answer. Jaxson saved me."

Bryson rolled his eyes.

"Check the rest of the footage. The hotel I can explain." She pulled her chair in, gripping the armrests. "Rhett gave me his credit card. I guess he thought it was romantic, but after all the crude comments he targeted towards me, I couldn't take another second. I tried, I really tried to be polite, but I couldn't do it. I walked out on him. I was going to press charges, but Jaxson stopped me—for this reason! How can a good man trust the law that is supposed to protect him, when you twist the truth for your own gain?"

She paused wondering how to explain the next bit, if she should quote Rhett's comments word-for-word, or simply state how violated they made her feel. By the expression on Bryson's face, he would've tuned her out, so she rambled on with the basics.

"Then he followed me and attacked me. Jaxson was only there because he promised to buy back Brooklyn's necklace his ex-friend stole. But it wasn't there; it was in the city, so I decided to go with him. The pawn shop was closed, and it was already really late. I still had the card on me, so I used it. Again, I used it, because I was angry. Jaxson found out and he made me stop. I'll pay it all back, but Jaxson didn't use the card. I did. If anyone should be in jail for theft, it's me."

Bryson's eyes widened. "No."

"Yes. The only thing Jaxson is guilty of is impulsively doing the right thing."

"Unfortunately the evidence points against him."

"Then find evidence that doesn't, like my testimony." She tugged on her hair, "Don't take him to court, Bryson. He can't afford it. You have to help me. You can't choose Rhett over your own family."

Bryson tapped the glossy surface of his desktop.

Melanie took a deep breath. "How did you know?" She tilted her head. "It was last night. How do you already have evidence? How do you already have a case against him?"

Bryson ignored her questioning, picking at his fingernails.

"If you can't do it for me, do it for Collette. You're going to ruin her wedding day. She made her decision to marry someone else, but she's really happy. If you care for her like you say you do, please, fix this."

He groveled, dropping the ballpoint pen.

"Do you want me to tell her you're the reason the best man—the groom's brother—couldn't show?"

"Don't." He glowered, seemingly more intimidating in his black suit. "Jaxson Thorne is a creature of habit. A liar, addict, thief, aggressor, and he is impulsive and manipulative. Two years ago, in the midst of a questionable relationship, he stole a ring. Again he possessed another ring with no proof of purchase. The man is dangerous and he is a criminal."

"Have you listened to a word I said?" Melanie yelped. She felt like she was talking to a brick wall. "What do you really have against him? Is it him or Jesse? You don't know what is best for me. You set me up on a date with a misogynistic creep. You think you can act as ultimate judge on a man's moral character, but that's not up to you." She shook her head. "You're flawed like the rest of us. You act self-righteous when you can't find love yourself. You hold on to this grudge that your ex moved on, and you're jealous that's she's happy with a man you don't like. Too bad. Why should that have any say on my relationship with Jax? Your inability to deal with your own demons is bringing us all down."

She slapped her palms on the table, "Look!" she shouted, "if you're mad at Collette, you need to talk to her. You can't change the fact she's getting married, but you can find resolution, you can talk this out, and you can forgive her. Live your life and move on." She took a deep breath, fighting the instinct to sob. She had to remain strong. "Stop using my fiancé to extract your revenge."

"He is not your fiancé!"

"He will be when you release him, or I'll tell Mom."

"You wouldn't."

"I will and I'll tell Grandma and Dad too."

Bryson clenched his fists, losing his resolve.

"Just fix this somehow and talk to Collette, not Jesse. You can't blame him for wanting to date her. Oh and don't tell her how you feel. This isn't about inflating your ego. Say what she needs to hear."

Bryson stood, turning his back to her. "Jaxson is a criminal."

"Was a criminal. People change. You have. Bryson, you used to be the biggest bookworm, a total loser, but a loser who was my best friend when I had none. When you met Collette she was extremely shy and introverted and it took us all by surprise when we found out you actually asked her out. Never had I thought I'd see you sneaking kisses with some stranger at a concert. People change. We hope for the better, and if not, we keep changing."

"If you knew Jax before—"

"And I don't. Thank goodness for that. I agree, I wouldn't like the old Jax, but he is a changed man. If it weren't for his past, he would have never wound up in the predicaments he had, eventually working for the Walters. And I may have never stumbled into him like I had." Her cheeks flushed remembering their first encounter—okay, maybe it was their second. She had worn the brand new shoes Bryson paid for, at a party he insisted she attend. "And as much as I hate to say this, I forgive you for locking him up. If he hadn't gone to jail, he may have never sobered up or flipped his life around for the better."

Bryson tipped his head in confusion, "Wait, do you want him locked up or not?"

"I want him here!" she screamed, biting her lip, regretting the volume she raised her voice to. "He doesn't need to suffer more, but give him a chance to prove himself. He will. Sometimes the greatest blessings, the longest strides, the moments of growth come not from the easy times, but when we're struck down, with nowhere left to go but up. He hit rock bottom two years ago. Having nothing shows us to appreciate something. The most successful men in the world learn from their failures. They strike gold when the cards are stacked against them, when the blessings run dry and they're cursed with the worst of luck, they look up. When they're stranded in the desert, they seek help. They stop blaming their situation and persevere in the hard times."

Bryson met her eyes momentarily, then turned away, clenching his jaw.

Melanie clasped her hands together. "That's why I love him. The world is against him, yet he drives all the way to the city to retrieve a necklace he didn't steal, and waits in the car until the shop opens, because he is that determined. He wants our respect, but he never demands it." Melanie took a deep breath, slowing down to steady her shaking body. Courage had a time limit and it was almost up. "He doesn't flick a credit card in a girl's face and demand a special payment plan."

"Hold on a second, Rhett would never..."

"Do you want the truth, or do you want to pretend you're right?"

"Then report him," Bryson said as if he was calling out a bluff.

"I promised Jaxson I wouldn't."

"You promised your 'innocent' boyfriend not to press charges on the person you claim to have assaulted and blackmailed you? Why would an innocent man let a criminal run free, especially one who attacked the person he claims to love? You need to press charges if you want a case. There's your truth."

Melanie's face fell into her hands and she wept. "The truth is I lied to you, Bryson. Dad cut me off after I had my driver's license revoked. I didn't sell those cars. I'm embarrassed I can't drive stick. He won't talk to me anymore and I don't know what I would do if you did the same. I don't know how Rhett knows, but he knows. You were wrong about him. I'd bail Jaxson out myself if I could, but I can't. If you can't clear his name, you can post his bail. Do it for me."

Bryson held his hand out, "Hold on. It isn't that simple."

"Um, he strangled my fiancé. Yes. I think it is."

He reached for his pen again. "He is not your—you've been dating for a month. Love isn't instantaneous." His grip tightened, baring his knuckles white.

"I can't wait to prove you wrong." She sniffed. "You'll find her, and you'll regret those words. Bryson, help me, help him. You're prosecuting the wrong man."

"Who is the lawyer, me or you?"

Melanie tilted her head in speculation, "He has something on you too, doesn't he?"

Bryson tapped the tip of his pen on his notepad again, forcing himself to not reveal any signs, but she knew. She wasn't the only one to have an eventful morning. Rhett had an inside on the law. He was rich and powerful, so it wouldn't surprise her if he dug dirt on her brother too. Rhett strangling Jaxson may have been the least of her worries. The dashing attorney was a malignant monster.

She placed her evidence, the black credit card on his desk. "Please, make him go away."

Chapter 15

"You're free to go," the officer said, handing Jaxson his belongings including the necklace. "Your charges have been dropped." Jaxson's neck was sore from two nights in the bunker. His eyes were dry and heavy, as the cell next to him had a talkative drunk each night. After shaking out his shoulders, he fished through the items, double checking everything was there, but it wasn't.

"Where's the ring?"

"This ring?" Bryson Duong had the velvet case open. He clapped it shut. "Pretty."

"Give it." Jaxson squinted, hastily picking up his step down the hallway.

Bryson bobbed his head side to side. "Why? So you can propose to my sister?" He peeked at the ring again. "Sapphire, neat touch." He rubbed his lips together. "You do realize what that will make us." Bryson tossed him the case.

Jaxson caught it with both hands.

"Brothers. If you marry my sister that will make me your older brother."

Jaxson looked across at him, raising an eyebrow at his cool composure. "And you're okay with that? You're not going to object?"

"How can I, when my sister is going around the whole town telling everyone you're already engaged? Have you had any success telling my sister no?"

"She is trouble."

"Yeah. Plenty." Bryson's nostrils flared as Jaxson passed him. "A thank you would be nice."

"Thank you for having me sleep two nights instead of one."

Bryson huffed, "Hey. Someone has to put you in your place. If you do anything, and I mean anything that negatively affects her well-being, I'll send you right back."

Jaxson smirked. "So what you're saying is, I have your blessing."

Her brother calmly slipped his hands into his pockets, then walked away. Rome wasn't built in a day. It took years for the Thorne brothers to sort out their differences, and Jaxson had no intention of going easy on his future in-law.

The wedding!

Jaxson looked up at the clock and his mouth went agape. He had less than four hours before Jesse finalized his vows.

He watched the needle on the speedometer religiously on the drive home, passing vehicles given any chance for a justified boost. As desperately as he wanted to speed, he couldn't afford a ticket or any reason to return to the station.

With less than an hour until the wedding, he ran into his house, gobbled down an unsatisfying peanut butter and jam sandwich, then jumped into the shower. He wanted to find Melanie, but Jesse would kill him on Collette's behalf if he stumbled in late. His nerves were shot. From the adrenaline of racing home and Bryson's bizarre change of heart, he let out a silent prayer.

Out of the shower, he slipped on a clean t-shirt and jeans, then squirted a few shots of cologne—a gift courtesy of Mrs. Walters' excessive shopping. Apparently, owning cologne was a male necessity. He left the baseball cap, but hooked his sunglasses on over his eyes.

He rushed to clip a bouquet of multicolored snapdragons, white roses, and pink tiger lilies, shoving them in the rinsed-out pickle jar from his kitchen counter. It was an impulse decision he hoped he wouldn't regret. There were a few smaller filler flowers shoved in, but he hadn't the time to add ribbons or make it appear as if he bought it.

Jaxson panicked. In his heart, Melanie came first, but Jesse was family and today meant so much to him. He rethought that, pulling out of the driveway. Their mother would always have a special place in their hearts, but they didn't have to be alone. He wondered if their mother would be proud of Jaxson's recent accomplishments and the man he became. He didn't have to resort to his imagination or be put down by lies. There was a woman present in his life who loved him unconditionally, who encouraged him to be a better man. She was beautiful and smart, innocent, and most of all, real.

Melanie had dropped off her wedding gift and the one from Bryson, adding it to the mountain of presents inside the church foyer. Her brother had been nowhere in sight, probably spending the morning in solitude somewhere, which seemed like the most appropriate course of action.

Nevertheless, she was a hot mess.

She put every effort into looking her best, but inside she felt miserable. She chose to wear a satin dress in a muted plum with a removable lacey bolero to cover her shoulders. Makeup couldn't mask the despair looming in her heart. Jaxson had spent two nights in the station jail and Bryson hadn't an inkling of compassion on him. She had to let go of the anger and focus on the positives. Her fury could wait one afternoon.

Melanie was ushered to a seat on the groom's side.

The ceremony was stunning, with flowers and ribbons everywhere. No one would suspect the ceremony was organized in under a month with Collette's superior planning skills. The piano playing in the background was delightful, yet it painfully reminded her of the duet she shared with Jaxson. Her heart had been conflicted. On one hand, he was the charming and romantic Carter, on the other he was the meddlesome yet outrageously attractive gardener with the vocal rasp of a rock star. When his icy edge melted, all that was left was fire, and the flames drew her in.

The minister walked down the aisle, then Jesse in his baby blue tuxedo which brought out soft chuckles from the crowd. She was impressed at how well he composed himself, considering his last remaining blood relative was locked up, and was going to miss this momentous occasion.

Trailing him was his brother in a navy suit.

Jaxson!

She covered her mouth in shock, unable to keep the tears at bay, as they gushed down her cheeks.

"We're next," he whispered as he passed her by, a smirk curling up his lip.

Jesse raised his brows, signaling for Jaxson to hurry up, and he did, tripping up the carpet steps. His brother caught him, then elbowed him jokingly in ribs. While Melanie couldn't hear what he said, she figured it was somewhere along the lines of "Bout time you show up," in a sarcastic tone. Jaxson in response shrugged unapologetically.

With the other two groomsmen joining them, they stood proud. The last one had swapped his bowtie for bolo tie, and his dress shoes for recently shined cowboy boots. She assumed Collette would not be impressed, but what could she do? Those four boys were a gang of rapscallions.

The bridesmaids were next. The second woman momentarily stole Jaxson's attention, he cricked his jaw and gripped his wrist tighter, wringing it to relieve the stress. They had a history. Melanie looked at the paper she was given with the wedding details. Her name was… Genesis. She quickly wiped her tears, then gave him a concerned look. The woman was stunning and seemingly his type. When his steel-blue eyes reconnected with Melanie's, he visibly relaxed and again winked at her.

They were in a room full of strangers, yet each glance to those eyes had her imagining ahead to their special day.

They were going to have a happily ever after. He wasn't going to spend another year or decades or whatever it may have been in jail. He would be sentenced to a lifetime of happiness with her.

Collette's mother walked down the aisle ahead of the three-year-old flower girl, offering encouragement as she threw handfuls of petals at random guests. Melanie figured it was a cousin or niece. She looked like a princess in her puffy dress with glittery butterflies, and the little tiara resting between her styled pigtails.

If Melanie was uncertain about kids before, this cutie-pie changed her mind in an instant. She needed a dozen of them stat. When her gaze returned to Jaxson, his grin widened. Could he read her mind? He said he couldn't, but there was a glint in his eyes that said otherwise.

Jesse was a sopping mess, pulling out the handkerchief in his tuxedo to wipe the flashflood of tears when his bride entered. Melanie wondered what Jaxson's reaction would be. She would have to work extra hard for a dream-like ceremony like this. She wouldn't rob Jaxson of her wedding dress moment, like Collette, who was in a snow-white mermaid style dress that accentuated her figure. She had lost weight since she dated Melanie's brother, but she still had her natural prominent curves, ones Melanie would never come close to having. Her golden curls were conditioned to bouncy ringlets.

Together Jesse and Collette had a notable height difference, except she couldn't help herself from admiring them. She glowed around him, and while Collette wasn't marrying her brother, Melanie would be marrying hers. Her mouth gaped. Why hadn't she thought about it before?

Collette would become her sister-in-law.

Jesse and Collette completed their vows, signed the legal document, then finalized the ceremony with a kiss. As their lips met, confetti burst into the sanctuary. Like a bomb, it shot out from all directions. Bits of glittery paper were everywhere. Jesse laughed, clearly surprising his wife with his scheme, then lifted her legs into the air, and carried her down the aisle.

Jaxson linked arms with Brooklyn, Ezekiel clasped hands with Genesis, brushing against her arm dotingly, and Grant raised his eyebrows at Stella, gesturing a 'ladies first.' She forced a smile, hooking arms with him at the furthest distance appropriately possible.

It seemed like forever for the guests to move. Melanie was stuck. She ducked her head in and out of the crowd, searching for Jaxson. Family and friends stood, chatting away, taking their sweet time to leave the sanctuary. People found her, sweeping her into conversation. Her leg was itching to get out of there. Half an hour must have passed, when the room had cleared enough for her to move freely.

A large hand covered her eyes. "Guess who?" he asked.

She pivoted in her step, and wrapped Jaxson into a hug. His suit jacket was off and he smelled delicious, whatever fragrance it was, she wanted more. He tipped down to meet her lips, but she pulled back.

"Not in a church."

Jaxson's eyes glinted with mischief, then he led her to his car, where he flicked on his sunglasses. She wanted to ask him about his dropped charges, who had bailed him out, or why on earth he was a free man and in the nick of time, but in the thick of it, she was overwhelmed he returned.

"I have something for you."

"You do?" she said, smirking cheekily. She held out her left hand, joking about the ring, except he handed her a bouquet. In the vase, which may have been a glass pickle jar, were white roses, pink tiger lilies, and snapdragons.

She flicked her gaze away, touched by the romantic gesture, except she found herself distracted by Bryson in his casual attire, a polo shirt and jeans, chatting with Collette. She shook his hand as he bit back a smile.

"Melanie?" Had Jaxson said something?

Bryson excused himself abruptly, rushing to his Audi to drive off.

"Mel?" Jaxson closed the distance between them, kissing a trail from her neck to her ear. His hot breath tickled her skin, "Will you?"

"Will I... what?" she asked.

Jaxson grinned at her hand, hanging his shades on his shirt. His eyes squinted from the bright skies, but she was certain there was another reason they were tearing up.

Melanie lifted it up, the pink rock shining in the sunlight.

"Will you marry me?"

Embarrassment tickled her cheeks pink. The answer was obvious and if she apologized for the recent distraction it would become a communication disaster.

"Big day," he sighed. "Sorry, it was an impulsive... I promised I wouldn't yet, but I had the ring, and I love you and I..."

Her arms wrapped around the back of his neck. She shut him up immediately, with a squeaky fun-loving smooch. He lifted her into the air, spinning her round and round as their lips danced with joy. His tears blended with hers.

"Yes," she mouthed.

A scream for joy startled them. It was Brooklyn. Her diamond necklace sparkled around her neck. How had Melanie not seen it before? She pointed towards them in the parking lot. "She said yes!"

"That's awesome, but we're going to be late for photos," Collette said, standing next to her sister. "Has anyone seen Grant or Stella?"

"Calm down, Lottie." Jesse kissed his wife's cheek, not surprised by the news. "Let them have their moment. He has worked really hard for this."

Jaxson turned to Melanie with an open palm. It was tanned and callused. He had healed gashes on his knuckles, and faint remnants of dirt stuck under his nails. He had worked hard. He had not a cent to his name, but he was rich in character, a son a mother would be proud of. He dug himself out of his own grave, so he could have a life, and he was choosing to spend the rest of it with her.

Melanie glanced at her partner from head to toe, and took his hand. They were in it for life.

Epilogue

"Okay. Open them."

She pulled Jaxson's hands away from her eyes to find a man slightly older than her, perhaps in his thirties, wearing a silk striped shirt and a thin gold chain around his neck. He looked like the Italian version of her brother with a similar hairstyle and dark eyes, only he seemed visibly more relaxed when he waved at her.

"What am I seeing?" She peeked at the rundown car the guy leaned against. With Jaxson's recent car purchase, it wasn't possible for him to impulsively buy her one, was it? Did he have to borrow money? It had only been two months since he popped the question. She wiggled the pink sapphire ring on her finger both confused and nervous. "What's going on?"

"That's Devon. He's a friend of mine."

"It's true," Devon said, "and he told me a certain someone needed help learning to drive."

"Oh, I can drive." Her body tensed. Jaxson had encouraged her to start the application process of regaining her license, but she figured having the card would be for the convenience of extra legal identity documents. "I just don't want to. I don't drive standard and maybe I should avoid the freeway, especially in the city." Plus she lived downtown, so nearly everything was walking distance.

Devon chuckled. These dirt roads were surrounded by thick lush forest. "No freeways around here." He threw her his set of keys. She missed, but Jaxson caught them, placing them in her shaking hands. "Not drinking behind the wheel is a given, and when you feel upset you should pull over, but I think the real problem is your driving confidence."

Melanie tugged on Jaxson's jacket, lowering her voice to a whisper, "Why are we doing this?"

"I can't drive you forever and as much as I love you, which is indefinitely, as is, you're not ready to borrow the Camaro when we're married."

Her eyebrows shot up. "Excuse me?"

Jaxson grinned. "But if it's October now and we're getting married in the spring. You will have plenty time to boost that confidence…"

"Fine." Her fingers curled into a fist over the keys. She hated that he knew she needed this, though she understood her man's love for his car. Jaxson babied the Camaro like Bryson his Audi. One day they would realize they had more similarities than differences.

"Enjoy your lesson." Jaxson kissed her goodbye on the cheek, then slid back into his vehicle. The leaves had fallen on the Walters' property and he would be preoccupied winterizing their gardens for another few days. "Dinner is on me tonight."

Devon opened the driver's side for Melanie. She buckled in, started the engine, and gripped the steering wheel for dear life.

"Don't go until you're ready," he reassured. Her fiancé's friend had a calming aura about him. That alone nearly put her at ease. "This is for you. Take a deep breath and focus on what you see, not the impending what-ifs, yeah?"

She inhaled recalling an emotionally lethal mixture of her worst moments, the cancer, the shouting of her parents, the first car hitting a barrier, the second sideswiping multiple vehicles like she had signed up for a demolition derby. She exhaled, returning to the present. A bird hopped from one side of the road to the other. Again, she slowly breathed in and out.

"What if I lose control?" The emotions she was worried about were from years ago, but what if they still held a tight leash?

"Pull over first."

"Right." She rolled her eyes. It was easier said than done. She signaled and steered the vehicle onto the dirt road. A few minutes down when they hit the poorly maintained pavement, she felt at ease enough to converse while driving. "You're really chill. You don't have to do this. Is Jaxson paying you?"

"I want to help." His phone rang and at the stop sign, she peeked at his lock screen. There was a freckle faced woman with thick glasses and a nervous grin. She had frizzy red hair and wore a turquoise sweatshirt that made her emerald eyes pop. From the pixels she could tell he had cropped a group picture to only show the two of them together. He stared at the man's name on his phone then rejected the call. "Eyes on the road."

"Right." She glanced at his phone again, but kept her foot firmly pressed against the brake pedal.

"You've been idling here for a while," he reminded her.

"No one is around. Who is she?"

"Drive," Devon requested gently. Following his directions, they entered town. "Valerie," he said after a few minutes.

"You like her?"

He smiled. "She's beautiful." If Melanie was allowed to check, she would have noticed the redness in his cheeks as he admired the woman through the image. "I'm going to invite her to our Halloween party."

"Ooh, break the ice?"

"Something like that. Will you and Jaxson be there?"

"I won't. I work that night and I have a feeling it's going to be a long shift." Melanie's eyes widened when she saw the Camaro parked across the street from her brother's apartment. Jaxson was leaning against the outside of his vehicle, pointing at the vacant parking stall behind him.

"Do you feel ready? Remember to signal."

"I know," she said, sticking out her tongue. She parked behind her fiancé's car with ease. Returning the keys, she caught him staring at his phone again. "Who was that on the phone?"

"Just family." He shook his head, showing he wasn't going to elaborate on the details. Boy, did she relate to the feeling of not wanting to talk to family. *La famiglia prima di tutto.* Everyone just getting into everyone else's business. Enjoy your date."

"Enjoy yours." Melanie smiled.

Devon's smirk faltered. There was something heavy on his mind, but if she was going to find out, it would have to wait for another day.

She raced to Jaxson's side and leaped into his arms.

"You're alive!" he teased. "I'm sorry I couldn't be of any help. I'd probably grab the wheel every two seconds." Or maybe it was the fact that if he was caught encouraging an unlicensed driver to take a turn behind the wheel, his criminal record would be further damaged. She understood and she appreciated the strings he pulled to help her out of this rut. He gave her a smooch on the lips, allowing it to linger. "And dang girl, you're better at parking than I am."

"It's just my nerves. I told you I can drive. I choose not to."

She watched Devon slide into the driver's seat of his car from the distance. He was red in the face, and with the door shut, he was screaming into the phone. His free hand whipped in various directions, overtly expressive to whatever had been bothering him—nothing like the calm and collected man she spent the last half hour with.

She turned toward Jaxson. "I'm choosing to drive safer, and that means I'm going to be the boss of my emotions, not the other way around." She took a deep breath, contemplating the steps she would have to take to accomplish her goal. "I want to belong on the road and I think that means I need to talk to my dad. There are things I need to work out."

Jaxson cupped her faced and kissed her again. "I'm proud of you."

She reached for his hand and pulled it down to her side. Together they crossed the street and walked the downtown perusing where to dine. "So Bryson's birthday is coming up."

"Am I supposed to buy him something? Ugh, there's Christmas too!" Jaxson's body stiffened. "If I find something cheap, it will be an insult. If I spend more money than I should, he's going to think I stole it."

"He isn't going to—"

"He is. But I can't get him nothing either. We're going to be brothers." He picked at his chin. It had been a few days since his last shave. She found the scratchy look irresistible. "And he doesn't have a sense of humor, so that's a no for gag gifts."

Melanie stood behind him and rubbed his shoulders. "Give him time. I know you two have bad blood, and I know you don't believe me when I say he was the fun one, but please be patient with him." She bit her lip, thinking of gift ideas, but she also was drawing up a blank. Since her brother was a minimalist with expensive tastes it was a challenge. "What if instead of buying something, you make—okay, maybe not make, but you could help him somehow."

A wide grin spread on Jaxson's face. "I have just the idea."

"What are you doing to my car?" Bryson freaked, charging down the stairs, not caring about his neighbors sleeping this late at night. He had skipped his jacket and the rest of his clothes were haphazardly slipped on. No socks for his shoes.

"Those are custom rims!" He curled his hand into a fist.

Jaxson finished removing the front tire on the driver's side, the tire iron still in his hand.

"Don't touch my car."

"But…" Jaxson's plan failed, as Bryson ripped the tool from his grip. "…Your birthday. I'm switching your tires for you. For winter."

"I don't need your help," he snapped, rolling the winter tire in position. "I don't need another Thorne touching my car."

"Bryson!" Melanie startled them, tugging on her brother's shirt. "Be nice. He didn't do anything wrong."

Jaxson rolled another winter tire closer to the summer one he had planned to swap out next.

"Don't touch my car. I had an appointment. I didn't need your fiancé to play shop boy."

"Do you know what you're doing?" Jaxson asked with concern leaking from his voice. He seemed to, but considering the value of his sports car, Jaxson didn't want to be blamed if his future brother-in-law messed up what he had already started.

"Of course I know to change a tire, but why should I when I can pay lowlifes like you to do it for me? You're robbing the mechanic of his business." Bryson's muscles flexed with each twist.

Jaxson looked over the Melanie and held up his hands in defense. "I tried."

Melanie sauntered over to him, shivering from the late night cold. Frost covered the ground and the autumn chill nipped at her skin. She wasn't dressed for the weather in her flannel shorts and that t-shirt she stole from Jaxson. He tugged her to his chest, sharing his warmth, and pulled her into a greeting kiss. Now that she was going to be forever his, he would never give up a chance to express his love.

"Bryson, you're being difficult," she said, afterwards, admittedly a little short on breath.

"I'm not being difficult. You're being unbearable." Her brother groveled, tightening the nut. "Insufferable! Both of you have some decency."

Jaxson raised his hand to her lower back. Perhaps they were a little carried away, but his woman was sensational and affectionate.

"We're getting married. Get used to it." Melanie stuck out her tongue.

"You're not married yet. Mel, a word."

Jaxson pointed up the stairs, as to meet him there when they were finished.

"No," Bryson said adamantly. "I can't stand you two. Yes, you're going to be husband and wife, but I don't want to see any of this." He motioned to them, referring to their affectionate behavior. "I don't like walking in on you. I live here too."

"Are you asking me to move out?" Melanie asked after Jaxson drove off. She was hoping for snuggles before he had to go, maybe while watching a movie.

"Yes," Bryson said hesitantly. He had persisted to finish switching out the last two tires. "You want me to like him, but every time I return home from work to find you locking lips, I… it ticks me off, okay? I need a break from you and you're lovey-dovey world. I forgave Collette, but I don't need daily reminders of the past. Pass me the nut."

Maybe it was best for the both of them, if she moved out of his apartment. Seasons change. She didn't need his company as much as she once had. Plus, if he ever pursued a relationship again, it would be awkward for her as the sister to witness if he brought his date home. Melanie picked up the small piece of metal and handed it to him.

"Since when have you known how to change tires?"

"Since always, Mel." Bryson sat down on the concrete barrier, to catch his breath. "Before you had cancer, before Dad moved to Hong Kong, we were a normal family, and we did normal things. I don't do them anymore, because I don't need to." He wiped the sweat off his forehead into his dark hair, pushing his overgrown bangs out of his eyes. "Just like you don't need to pay for your wedding. Talk to Dad. You shouldn't have to dump your savings for your big day. To him, it's a drop in the bucket, heck the ocean."

"I know Dad is rich now."

"Yeah, but I don't think you realize how rich. He hasn't cut you off. He is hesitant because you cut him off, but you'll always be his princess." Bryson crouched to the final tire, tightening the last bolt. "He's not a millionaire. His fortune has more than tripled. He has an empire over there. Do you understand? Dad is officially a billionaire."

"He asked you to move to Hong Kong again, didn't he?"

Bryson nodded with a solemn expression on his face.

"Don't follow in his footsteps," she pleaded. "What if you fall in love? If you copy him, you won't gain. You will work and work and work until you die. You can't have both."

Bryson clenched the tire iron, making a fist. "But I won't fall in love."

"You will." She wrapped her arms around her brother and gave him a tight squeeze. "You will fall in love again. You will be happy. You will find purpose. Don't give up. Not for money, not for anything. Promise me." She held out her pinky.

"Pinky promises aren't legally binding."

"Promise!"

Bryson rolled his eyes. She insisted, so he lifted his pinky finger and hooked it onto hers.

Bryson Duong is next in _the Lovelorn Lawyer._

He fell in love,
but she only needed his help.

Bryson Duong is an unstoppable prosecutor, winning case after case in court. He firmly believes the guilty must be punished according to the law, except the brute who wronged his pro-bono client dies unexpectedly, leaving Valerie, a pregnant woman, financially stranded.

Lonely and attracted to her kindness, he offers to take on the responsibility of supporting her and her awaited child through a marriage in name, a name secretly worth well over a billion dollars overseas. With one of the most romantic days of the year around the corner and pressure from his family, could she become his Valentine?

Acknowledgements

My real inspiration for Jaxson wasn't his level of hotness, but a true story about a felon who cleaned his life up. I don't know the person personally, but he became a Christian, got married, started a family, but to officially be considered a free man (I'm not American, I don't understand the system in USA), he needed the "forgiveness" of the person he wronged. That person held the grudge and therefore restricted the livelihood of the felon. While it's fun to salivate over hunks, I hope the take home here is how important it is for us to forgive those who have wronged us.

Round of applause for my beta readers Johanna Evelyn and E.C. Fountain, and my editor Lisa Lee! A special shout out to my husband, and his amazing biceps that I not-so-secretly admire when he works around the property. He's mine, you can't have him!

When you write a review, it makes a world of difference for us indie authors. Go for it! All it takes is a few seconds. It helps us continue to create the stories you love.

Happy Reading!

-Ria Zen

About the Author

Ria lives in Northern British Columbia. She enjoys the small-town charm with her handyman husband and children. She tends to geek over superheroes and cartoons. When she isn't writing or addressing immediate mothering tasks, she often returns to a life of home renovations and to her beloved sewing machine.

Amazon: Ria Zen
Bookbub: Ria Zen
Facebook: Ria Zen
Goodreads: Ria Zen
Instagram: @riazen.author

www.ingramcontent.com/pod-product-compliance
Lightning Source LLC
Chambersburg PA
CBHW030930060726
47591CB00005B/1738